LUNA STATION
QUARTERLY

Issue 052 | December 2022

The Tree Issue

Editor-in-Chief
Jennifer Lyn Parsons

Editors
Anna Catalano • Bridget Siniakov • Cait Ryan
Carly Racklin • Cathrin Hagey • Izzy Varju
Katrina Carruth • Katrina Schroeder • Sara Doan
Sarah Pauling • Shana Ross • Gô Shoemake

LUNA STATION PRESS
NEW JERSEY

First Paperback Edition December 2022
ISBN: 978-1-949077-38-4

Luna Station Quarterly publishes short fiction on March 1st, June 1st,
September 1st, and December 1st. For more information and submission
guidelines, please visit our website at lunastationquarterly.com

For Luna Station Press

Creative Director—Tara Quinn Lindsey
Editor-in-Chief & Founder—Jennifer Lyn Parsons

LUNA STATION PRESS

www.lunastationpress.com

CONTENTS

Editorial

Elizabeth Hinckley

As a naturalist and an author, Elizabeth Hinckley has a passion for both the natural world and the power of story, and their ability to inspire the human spirit. She is the author of David, A Rat. She lives in New Jersey, home to a surprisingly beautiful and diverse array of natural wonders, which she explores frequently.

Once upon a time, I lived in an apartment where I was unhappy. Unlike my previous home, where I could walk out the back and wander meadow and forest for miles, this apartment was in an industrial town next to the stripped hillside and constant booming of a quarry. In our second floor apartment, the concrete postage stamp of a yard behind the house was really only accessible by the downstairs neighbors, but it was only a little fenced in garbage depot anyway, so we were cut off from that much-needed connection with something green and living. Except for the single big beautiful tree that grew there.

That tree helped keep me connected during that time. We didn't know how long we'd be stuck in that place, but over the course of a few years, I watched the tree out of the back window as it transformed that small space into another world. At my second floor height, I felt like I was in its canopy during the warm months, enveloped in a lush green ball of life. Each branching pattern created a three dimensional world which filled the space with a neighborhood for urban wildlife. The birds and squirrels did not move side to side, they moved between different levels of their living skyscraper, tending to their important daily matters. In the winter, after the leaves had fallen and I could see through to the apartments behind, it took some imagination to envision the huge world the tree occupied during the summer; it had been reduced somewhat to scaffolding, but it was still beautiful in its skeletal elegance, and I knew that its secret world would return again. That tree was a keystone, a safe space, in a place where I needed it the most. When we finally moved, I knew I would not see it again and said goodbye, knowing that like the squirrels and birds, my time with it was a small part of its lifetime.

In my work as a naturalist, I found the words to describe things I intuitively knew about forests and trees. When I knew nothing about them, I could still tell you how a forest "felt" to me, without the designations I learned: the look of an upland oak/beech forest, or the quiet of a hemlock grove, with the sound muffled by the soft duff of needles underneath your feet. I was able to go from a holistic emotional feeling about a group of trees, to identifying how the individual species differed, back to how they all interacted to form a forest ecosystem. In effect, I learned to read the forest like one learns how to read words, and it enriched my understanding. But I never, ever, want to forget how they feel, even when you don't know their names.

Each of the writers in this issue, and each of you reading, has some connection to trees like this—I'm sure of it. Unless you live in Svalbard, or a desert, its highly unlikely that you haven't felt the pull and magic of trees. (Besides, living in a treeless environment doesn't mean you've never heard of or seen a tree!) It's universal, and likely built into our DNA the same way that the sound of trickling water soothes us. Trees make a small world big, and put our human concerns in perspective: when human stuff seems like the most important thing in your world, try going outside and listening to birds in trees. The meaningless chatter supplying the background to your day is a whole culture happening right above your head, as different individuals share the news of the day, create relationships, and live life to the fullest. Meanwhile, the 'neighborhood' under their feet is a living partner, witnessing generations of comings and goings as it provides everything they need.

Trees live their lives on a different scale, and we poetically imbue them with traits we examine in ourselves. This does not, by any means, imply that they lack these traits. When our story trees talk or move, express feelings, wrestle with immortality, nurture others, or hold the secrets of life, they may not literally do it in the same ways they do in what we perceive as 'regular life'—the stories just help us to see ourselves a little better, and imagine the ways that they can. And make no mistake, they can. Look for them the next time you spend time with a tree, on the tree's terms. Take time to think three dimensionally and over a lifespan longer than ours.

And now...enjoy this issue, perhaps while leaning up against a tree, or twirling a leaf between your fingers.

L S Q | 052

Spruce and alder—Maple and pear
All lament that there are few who

remember the old *hardingfele* dances
lost in the journey across the sea

"It's just you and me now", said the
puppeteer to his oldest friend

who picked up his tiny fiddle, tuning
it to the birds and the wind, before

playing an old *slattar*, sympathetically
to the children gathered beneath

the trees at the edge of the park
Spruce and alder—Maple and pear

All keepers of memory, and elegy
and *bygdedans*, as time winds down

- Tara Quinn Lindsey

The Warrior Tree

Chana Kohl

From the moment I was born, my parents knew I would need to fight to find my place in this world. That is why they named me Faiza. The victorious one.

Ten perfect fingers and ten perfect toes—it's what every mother checks when they see their newborn the first time. But when the midwife brought me to my mother, she felt the universe pivot. She said it was something in the way the old woman's eyes refused to meet hers.

I was born with ectrodactyly.

Taking me into her arms, my mother examined for herself my tiny hands—thumbs but no fingers—stretched up towards a world that would recoil from them. She looked into my eyes, too innocent to understand the guilt and shame she would endure silently, needlessly because of me.

Still, my mother told me she fell in love the instant she held me.

I was born during the most festive time of the year in Morocco, so my father, a sheep farmer, slaughtered a ram the day I was born, sharing it with our neighbors, and then another seven days later. He knew raising a girl, his only daughter, with different needs and appearance would be a burden in our remote village. Still, he was thankful. The 'Years of Lead' were evaporating, a new century and political reforms were on the horizon. He always told his children anything was possible.

Wedged between the rain shadow of the Anti-Atlas and the salt lick of the Sahara, the tiny, Amazigh village where I grew up lay next to fields of saffron stretched under lucerne skies. Most men eked out meager livelihoods from saffron, olives, and cereal wheat between the years of drought. It was beginning to exact a toll: the 'dry years' seemed to come more frequently and last longer.

The women, in contrast, were master carpet weavers. Known from Agadir to Marrakech for their nimble skills, they passed this sacred tradition from mother to daughter, encoded in their maternal DNA. But not my DNA.

When I turned sixteen, a time when most girls proved their feminine virtues by sitting at the loom and learning intricate patterns, or working in the argan collective with lightning-quick fingers, I worked and tended the fields. Several crops were needed for dyeing carpet wool: madder, indigo, and turmeric. Caring for the plants, from the time they were furrowed until they were ready to harvest, made me feel useful to my family. That was important to me. So while some of the older women sat and gossiped, combing and spinning strands of wool for dyeing, I watered and weeded, coaxing my delicate flowers to bloom.

And this is what I hoped I'd do for the rest of my days. At least until the day my father came from Tiznit with news that would change my life forever. I saw him walking towards me in the field and knew exactly what he was going to say.

"Who?" I asked.

***

I sat beneath an old argan tree. It swayed and bowed from the desert headwinds, but never completely buckled. Hot, salty tears left their streak marks down my face. I planted my hands in the rocky soil, wishing I was the one who could take root.

The feeling my family was abandoning me—finally throwing off the burden they received the day I was born—sat on my chest like a heavy stone. My mother came and sat down beside me. "It's natural to be afraid," she wrapped her arms around me, "so was I when the time came to marry your father."

My head rested on her bosom as I spent those last moments of my childhood listening to her calming words. The same balm mothers soothed their daughters with since betrothals began. I wondered how many times those same words had been whispered beneath those branches.

"Sometimes we don't have a choice in the matter, but it does not mean you won't grow to love him." I wondered how she could be so sure. My parents knew each other their entire lives. From the time my father finished school, there was never any question they'd end up together. "It's not as if he is very old," she explained. "These days, forty-two is still considered young for a man."

In my mind, he might as well have been ninety.

"The most important thing is that he has a job and he can take care of you, Faiza."

At this, my head raised, prepared to voice the protest building inside. "So you admit it?"

"Admit what?" My mother was genuinely confused. Maybe

she thought I'd be happy or relieved they found someone for me to marry.

"That the reason you're sending me away to live with a man, a widower I've never met, whose children are older than I am, is because of money? If we were richer, I could go to school, like girls in Rabat. Maybe even attend a university?"

I had always excelled in school, but like most girls in my village, I stopped at 8th grade. Depending on the family's straits, some quit even earlier. But my oldest brother Adil was a carpet trader in Marrakech, where he said it was acceptable, even considered normal, for girls to attend high school and sometimes beyond that.

"Where are you getting these ideas? Girls in the city have lower moral standards. Hassan Hadid will make a good husband and needs a good, devout wife!"

"And what about these?" I raised my arms and showed her the hands that were given to me. The only hands I'd known, the hands that always invited stares, the ones I always tried to hide. Would my new husband be ashamed of them also?

"He knows about your condition and doesn't object. This is important. You want a husband who will treat you with respect. He will treat you well because his business prospects depend on it."

And that is when I knew the man they'd chosen for me did not really want to marry me. Only my family's wool. "Please, don't make me do this," I begged her.

"Faiza, it's time you grow up and face reality. The weaving cooperative will never take you and you cannot work in these fields forever. This is the best option. Or would you rather move to the city and work as a maid? Do you know what happens to your reputation if you do?"

I knew my parents were doing what they thought was best. I did not argue with her. It wasn't as if I didn't know this day might eventually come. What I did not know was how far I would go to resist.

**

Standing outside Dr. Yosef Ouaknine's door, I inched closer to Adil. My hair, scrubbed, brushed, and twisted at the nape, smelled of cardamom and amber beneath my headscarf. I had borrowed my sister-in-law's *abaya* to wear and, despite the intense heat, wore a long-sleeved tunic beneath it that fell past my hands. We decided on the way that Adil would do all the talking. I hoped the professor, one of Adil's customers, would not notice me there at all.

A man, tall but slightly stooped, answered the door and welcomed us in. Judging from his copious silvery hair, he was somewhere in his sixties. He invited us into his study for mint tea.

My jaw fell when I entered. I couldn't help it, I had never seen such a room. Almost every wall housed books from floor to ceiling. The one wall that didn't, the one behind his desk, had shelves of glass jars instead, each labeled in Arabic and filled with plant specimens: hundreds of seeds, shoots, dried piths, and hulls.

He thanked a middle-aged woman, Farah, who came and set a tray of tea and glasses on the low table in front of us. Her eyes lingered on my long sleeves as she looked at me suspiciously. I was afraid to reach for it. Instead, I folded my arms on my lap and let it grow cold.

"So your brother tells me you want a job working in my argan orchards." He spoke softly as if even the walls were listening. Perhaps they were, Farah was just outside the doorway, still, his voice made me feel at ease. "I have to be honest with you, this is hard work you're seeking. I really expect to hire a man for this job." He glanced towards my sleeves. I'm certain Adil already told him about my difference. "As you can see, I already have a maid."

My brother mounted a defense. I could always count on him. Even when I told him I needed to find honorable work in the city so I could get out of my arrangement, something that would allow me to live, even save money to send back to our parents, he did not turn me away.

'Faiza already tends the fields in our village. She knows a lot about plants, and don't be fooled, she's very strong for her size. The best thing is," he added, his voice rising so Farah could easily hear, "she won't bring you any trouble. All she does at home when she's not working in the fields, or helping my mother in the kitchen, is read whatever books she can find."

My brother was good at persuasion. There was a reason he could sell so many carpets.

Over eager to help, I added, "Back home I used to throw stones at the branches, gather the nuts when they fell. We'd crack and roast the pits to grind with orange honey and cinnamon."

I regretted speaking even before the last word.

Dr. Ouaknine looked at me, squinting. His hazel eyes had flecks of yellow, like the pith of an argan seed ready to pick. "You know, Faiza, what we do here at the agricultural college is not the same as growing trees for nut butter in your backyard. Come with me, both of you. Let me show you."

He brought us to an outer courtyard, down stone steps to an open field. Most of the trees grew in containers but one, like a sultan's guard, grew directly from the ground.

"Its scientific name, Faiza, is *Argania spinosa*. I sometimes call it the giant relic of the Maghreb as it's quite a stubborn son of a bitch. They can live for hundreds of years, but Southern Morocco has lost more than 50% of its argan forest in the last ten years alone. The government has funded me to figure out a way to reverse this."

As we walked through the field, he explained how each row of trees were identical copies of an original tree and how he planted them in different soils. He showed me how it was done. He took a small pocket knife and cut deftly into the bark of a branch, wounding it, and covering it up, he tied it with a bag of soil. He pointed to my hands, "Do you believe you can do that?"

I looked at Adil. We had lost.

Later in the car, he spoke softly as he drove me back to the train station, "I don't believe marrying Hassan will be as terrible as you think." Then he kissed me on my forehead.

There was going to be a wait before my train arrived and Adil had to get back to the shop, so he gave me enough money for lunch and a Coca-Cola and left. As I sat in the train station, I watched people arriving and departing. I wondered how many of them had control of where they were going. Were any of us truly able to choose our own destination? How many just sidled along tracks already laid down for them?

It was at that moment I got up from my seat and walked out of the train station, back to the main road. At first, I didn't know where my feet were heading. Later I realized I was walking back towards the college campus, all eight miles. I didn't stop until I reached the professor's door. When I knocked, Farah answered.

She did not look impressed.

She told me Dr. Ouaknine was having his supper and was not to be disturbed. I told her that I'd wait and that I already missed the last train back to Agadir. Temporarily homeless and possibly out of my mind, I looked her in the eye and told her I had to speak to him again, If I went back now, there was just one option waiting for me.

She shook her head and told me to wait in the study.

I waited for what seemed like hours, then the professor came and sat down across from me. "This is highly unusual. I thought I explained to you, Faiza, I don't believe the work is suitable for you." Still, he listened.

I asked him for just one chance to prove I could do the work. If I couldn't learn it then I'd go back to my family. Farah stood in the doorway, listening. She looked at her employer. I knew the look all too well and I hated it. It was the look of low expectations from an unwanted burden.

Dr. Ouaknine recognized the look also, but instead of asking me to leave, he walked to one of his many bookshelves and retrieved a book. Then he asked, "Did you finish high school?"

I wanted to scream. How could I explain that I stopped my studies because I had no choice, "No," I said looking at the book, "but I do read Arabic."

He opened it to a page and asked me to read it for him. It was about a monk in Austria who worked in a garden, counting peas, and how it led to an important discovery. Then he explained how significant this simple work would become to the field of genetics.

"Tell your brother, Faiza, I think you're extremely brave to come back here on your own and plead your case. I'll give you a chance to prove you can do the work. And if you work here, I expect you to continue your studies. You have a lot of catching up to do."

He asked if my parents approved of me staying in Marrakech. I told him yes.

I lied.

***

The next day, I rose before dawn. A small lamp next to the bed I had slept in cast an uneven light on my surroundings. A storage cabinet, its paint curling fruitlessly from the wood beneath, hung over the door. It was empty, except for a few books with drawings of trees. Farah said it was just a dorm room for students, but I felt it was created just for me.

The feeling of unknown possibilities was a strange, heady elixir in my veins. It traveled like wildfire towards my chest, ravaging it completely, and left me with only embers—both of anticipation and dread. I had called Adil the night before. I told him how I couldn't get on the train and that I wanted to live and study in Marrakech. I begged him to convince our parents the work was respectable and to let me stay.

He said he'd try, but he didn't sound too hopeful about it.

I finished my list of chores before the sun finished moving from softly golden to harsh and white. The work was no different from what I did at home: mopping floors, washing clothes, hanging them to dry. Afterward, Farah prepared us a morning meal of bread, covered with *amlou*, and soft, white cheese with dates, then I followed the professor into the orchard.

"This entire row needs to be cloned," he said, pointing towards a row of thirty trees, tagged and growing in pots. He explained how to choose the best branches to wound, then showed me how to apply a solution and sphagnum moss to help it take root. I rolled my sleeves. He made it look effortless, yet it took me several attempts just to make a single notch. It wasn't pretty, but it helped to steady the gnarled and thorny branches with my bared teeth.

By noon, I had scrapes and cuts all over my arms, but I finished more than half the trees. Farah watched me occasionally from the kitchen window. She called for me at lunchtime, shaking that head. She seemed worried or, more probably, confused. I don't think she understood why a young woman would choose such unseemly work.

Looking back, I'm not sure that lunch really happened, or if it was just a dream, a single moment stretched to infinity in my mind. The professor talked about the trees, his work in the Negev, and a host of other topics I could barely understand. But I nodded as if I did. It was clear how much saving the argan from extinction meant to him and he seemed pleased with what I had managed to do so far.

So when I saw my brother's car pull up outside, I wasn't alarmed. It was natural he'd check on me, to see for himself what I was up to. But when I saw my father and my mother get out of the car, my heart froze. Then it fled. I looked at the clock on the kitchen wall: they must have taken the first train out of Agadir.

My father's eyes were brimming with barely controlled rage. I knew he was ready to grab me if I refused to go back and my mother would allow it. I was only glad he didn't take it out on Dr. Ouaknine. My father didn't want trouble, he only wanted what was rightfully his to protect.

"Faiza, you need to come now," he didn't even look in Dr. Ouaknine's direction. My mother stood with her hands folded, but her eyes implored me not to resist. It was then I knew there were never any other tracks for me to choose. They all led to the same place. I looked over at Adil and I saw for the first time: he knew all along. He just didn't have the courage to tell me the truth.

Or maybe he just wanted me to figure it out for myself.

It seems so strange now, what I was thinking. Maybe everyone has that moment in their youth, where the world seems to balance on a fine line of persisting or ending, the point in time when you must decide where your family ends and you begin. But for the first time in my life, I felt there was something I–Faiza, had to do.

I turned and walked away from my brother's car. I grabbed the professor's pocket knife and headed toward the orchard.

"Faiza!" I heard my father call after me. Then I heard my mother's footsteps follow me as she placed her hand on my arm. She tried to stop me from going another step, but I yanked it away. The tears finally burst their dam.

"Let me finish!" I yelled at her. I didn't care about anything else, I just kept walking. I looked over my shoulder and saw my father rush at me. My mother held him back.

"Just wait," she told him quietly, "she'll come."

I don't know why my parents allowed me that one thing, maybe they never saw me defiant before, or maybe they thought, after everything, I deserved a chance to prove myself, but they waited until I finished the entire row. The sun was powerful and relentless that time of day and there was no shade. At one point, Dr. Ouaknine came to me and told me not to worry about the trees, to let it go, that he'd finish the work himself.

Didn't he understand? "I said I would do it! Is it too much to give me that?" And I added so that only he could hear, "Please let me finish this. Then you'll never have to see me again."

Not yet to the end of the row, my ears were ringing, and my breaths came short and quick. I was scared I would pass out. Farah brought me water from the garden pump, holding it while I drank. The water was warm as tea as it ran out and past the sides of my mouth.

She mopped the sweat streaming down my face, stinging my eyes, "You should listen to your family," she told me. "They know what's best for you." I knew that. Still, I shook my head.

My hands and arms were a bloody mess by the time I finished. I collapsed into my mother's arms, crying, as she led me back to the car. Before I knew it, I was on the last train back to Agadir.

Three years later, I was living in Tiznit with a family of my own.

***

I held my infant son in one hand while my two-year-old daughter reached up to grab the other. Together we walked through the small garden I had slowly built. There were almond saplings, miniature orange trees, and, of course, a wild, argan tree just starting to spread its arms and offer shade. My daughter especially loved dipping her fingers in the fountain pool Hassan placed at the center of it all.

My husband had a gentle spirit. I was lucky. I took care of him and he gave me the honorable life my parents wanted. My family had made certain.

The three of us sat on a wooden bench waiting for Uncle Adil who came regularly to visit on business. He always brought something for the children, but on that day, he had a packet for me. It was from the professor, a book, the one I read aloud in his study three years ago.

"Dr. Ouaknine still comes by the *souk* every so often," Adil explained. "He's glad you're doing well. Last week he asked if I would give this to you."

I had thought about that day in the orchard, usually in the early hours, before the children were awake and when the light made everything so vague. Still, it seemed so long ago. When I opened the book, I saw a message he'd written inside:

Faiza —

I wanted you to have a memento of your brief visit to the college. It's no coincidence: the thirty trees you propagated not only surpass every metric but are doing so in every soil I have planted them. These trees seem to be every inch the determined warrior as you so, from henceforth, will be a new cultivar called A. Spinosa 'Faiza.'

I closed the book with a small laugh. It felt odd reading those words, almost as if they were written about someone in a storybook, not me. I never wanted to be a warrior. That was never my dream as a little girl, climbing trees like a goat just to see how far I could see. I went to Marrakech because I wanted to choose my own path. What I needed was to find that part of myself that was my own.

The truth is no tree chooses its own soil. If those trees become warriors, it's because they will find whatever they need from what they already have.

***

"Oxygen concentrations are rising, slowly, but well beyond the confidence interval of Phase I levels alone," Dr. Ayalah Zeyad's recorded voice relayed the same childlike exuberance she felt the first time her boots touched Martian soil.

Far beneath the planet's surface, soft fluorescent light bounced through LED pipes and spread throughout inflatable greenhouses. Standing like sentries, hundreds of *Argania spinosa* were monitored for growth and respiration. She re-checked the numbers in her scientific log. If the measurements were correct, the trees had adapted to the Martian regolith beautifully.

Given their provenance, she wasn't surprised.

The Martian Ecological Development project was a major part of NASA's Phase II habitation schedule. Tasked with creating a sustainable environment in the underground habitat ring, they were now weaning the controlled atmosphere from electrolysis and oxygen scrubbers to a biological system: the first step, a baby one, towards a sustainable colony on Mars.

"The primary specimens are a stress-resistant cultivar of *Argania spinosa* developed by Dr. Yosef Ouaknine in the early 2000s. The species, one of the few botanicals to survive the Pleistocene, evolved as the last green defense against the encroaching Sahara. I believe it may be our best candidate for the ring and possibly bioconversion of Martian soil."

Ayala stopped the recording and set the data pad on her desk. Above it, preserved in an acrylic case and mounted on the wall, lay the browned and tattered pages of a genetics book long bereft of its binding. The words on the first page, however, were clearly visible: a small note of appreciation, scribbled by Dr. Ouaknine's own hand, and given to her great, great grandmother, Faiza Hadid.

Shadow and Ash

Sarah McPherson

Sarah McPherson loves folk tales and myths and finding the weird in the everyday. Her flash/short fiction has been widely published, nominated for Best Small Fictions, longlisted for the Wigleaf Top 50, and selected for Best Microfiction 2021. Find her on Twitter as @summer_moth or at https:// theleadedwindow.blogspot.com/.

You have been walking for weeks, or at least that's how it seems. Your feet hurt, your back hurts, your heart hurts. More than anything you want to stop, but the sense of something behind you drives you ever onwards. It's not a higher purpose propelling you forwards, but a presence, some malign entity, just out of sight when you glance behind. Nonetheless, you know it is there.

You're not sure how long it has been following you, you only know that it has been days, many days now since you first became aware of it. Constant, too far away to perceive with your physical senses but close enough to feel in your very bones. You don't know what it wants but it cannot be anything good.

You have passed through several villages, but you don't dare to stop, even for a single night. It wouldn't be safe. You can't say quite what you fear would happen, but you know in your heart that something dreadful would happen, maybe to you, maybe to those who shelter you. And so, you keep walking.

It, whatever it is, grows closer every day. You still can't see it, but you know. You can't escape its presence but still, you keep moving. There is nothing else to do. A few times the notion of sitting and waiting for it occurs to you–it might be better than this inexorable forward motion--but your mind shies away from what might happen if you were to come face to face with it. And so you walk.

One morning, perhaps the fifteenth day, or the fiftieth, as the sun rises in the sky towards noon, you come to a stand of ash trees. Very old, they are. They were here before this road, for it swings to the side and arcs around them.

As soon as you step into their circle you feel it. Life. There is such life here. It is ancient, and it is deeply rooted and strong. So strong. It seeps into you and pushes the fear that you only now realize has been consuming you out to the edges of your consciousness. Your resolve strengthens and you feel certain if there is anywhere you can make your stand it is here, in this ring of trees.

You sit on the grass, your back against one broad trunk, and close your eyes and for the first time in an age, sleep comes easy. You do not dream, or if you do you hold no memory of them, and when you awaken the afternoon shadows are lengthening and the sun is low in the cloudless sky. Your mind feels rested, and yet you are acutely aware of the aching of your body. Muscles, bones; every joint is a complaint.

You pull yourself to your feet and as you do the wind catches the trees and a cascade of seeds rain around you. Tiny winged keys sail down, joining those that already litter the ground. One lands softly in your outstretched palm and you curl your fingers around it, solid and yet so fragile.

You slip the seed key into your pocket and look around. It feels safe here, inside this cluster of trunks, and yet somehow you know that once you step outside the feeling of dread, of pursuit, will return. And you have wasted so much time here already, resting. You wonder what you can possibly do to end this, for you cannot continue this way for much longer.

As the sun sets and the shadows stretch out long fingers, your eyes come to rest on a crack in the bark of the tree opposite you. Unbidden, your hand returns to your pocket and you draw forth the seed. The key. The crack is a dark hole in the trunk, a fissure, small and deep. The seed key slips into it as though the two were made for each other. Although it feels brittle in your fingers, you trust that it will not break as you turn it clockwise and feel, rather than hear, a click within the tree.

Nothing changes. Nothing that you can see. The trees loom around you, as they must have for hundreds of years. The darkness continues to descend. But you feel it again. Life, swelling and swirling and flowing around you. It enters you, fills you, invigorates you. The aches and pains that seemed all-consuming recede, replaced by a sense of well-being and happiness that you have not felt in who knows how long. Light--not visible, but a feeling of lightness--surrounds you.

And that's when you see it; billowing over the horizon and bearing down on you with unimaginable speed, for the first time you actually see it. Black and nebulous. More shadow than form. A cloud, a patch of shade, with no more than a hint of limbs and body and head. There are no features that you can make out but you feel its gaze nonetheless. You feel its desire.

You ought to feel fear, now, at last, seeing it there in front of you. But you don't. The feeling of lightness that you unlocked from the trees is still with you, sustaining you. You gaze at your shadow, revealed finally in the twilight, and, eyeless, it gazes back.

Some instinct tells you that the light of the trees can hurt it if you can only find a way to use it. It takes you a moment, but when realization strikes it is so obvious you almost laugh. The trees are strong and sturdy, but any wood has deadfall and this one is no exception. It doesn't take you long to gather a small pile and a matter of moments to call forth a spark from your flint and steel.

The flames leap up from the dry heap you have prepared, dancing and twisting and bright, so bright. Your shadow, whatever it is, recoils from the glow. You shore up your little fire, feed it, nurture it. Give it all your attention so you don't feed the dark spirit that watches you without a face. The circle of light you have created grows and expands, and the shadow throws back its featureless head and lets out a howl, like nothing you have ever heard.

As the sound dissipates, so too does the creature itself, blown like smoke on the wind, like wisps of fog in the morning. And the feeling of dread that has been squatting in the back of your mind goes with it, and you feel free for the first time in a long time. You lie down by the side of your fire, and let its warmth seep into you, and sleep.

Lost and Found; Retreat and Return

Emma Schmid

Emma Schmid lives in London, Ontario with her family and failed service dog trainee, Frea. She is currently working on a Certificate of Creative Writing through the University of Toronto. When she's not writing, Emma enjoys watching K-Dramas, playing Animal Crossing, and trying to get through a to-be-read stack the size of a small dog.

The boundaries of Bea's haven were clear, though they remained unseen.

A small shimmer in the air, the smell of sulfur stuffing itself up her nose—these markers told her she was getting too close to the edges. Though she hadn't seen another human in at least 200 years, she was still wary of getting too close—of seeing something she didn't want to.

Of being seen.

Since the cliff's edge, Bea didn't practice magic much. Her haven provided her the necessities—the clever little spell was one for bounty and boundary; easily confused with the spell for misery and disorientation.

Not that practicing mattered much; her bookshelf was stocked, her pantries full. The only thing she missed, she realized as she stood at the boundary, inhaling the smell of rotten eggs, was people.

The trees provided her cover, offering companionship in the form of listening ears. It really was too bad that they couldn't talk back. In her head they did. In her head, Bea and the trees had long, rich conversations about the books she read and the animals that crossed the boundary of her haven freely. She'd taken to naming them—the animals—but could never tell if they were the same. They stayed far from her when they came into her clearing—animals didn't like the sulfurous smell of magic that lingered around her; an after-effect of keeping the boundary spell in place.

She'd been able to feel the trees since she was a young girl, when the entire forest had been her playground. Her affinity for greenery allowed her to feel the roots beneath her feet, to sense the rustling of the highest branches...until she cast her spell.

Now, as she stood at the boundary, the second time already that day, though it was barely dawn, she felt the edge of the boundary like a physical wall between her and the trees. Beneath her feet, the root systems stopped; cut off completely, though she knew it couldn't be possible.

Like an extension of herself, the spell informed her of the happenings in her haven, which included even the leaves that dropped to the ground in the autumn. She'd know if a trees' roots had suddenly been cut off, or stopped growing.

No, this was the boundary reminding her that she was like the roots of the trees—a part of her belonged to the rest of the forest, though she couldn't reach it.

But if I left...

Everyone she knew was dead. Her parents, her aunts...the friends she'd had in the hamlet for a brief time. Bo. After 200 years, there couldn't possibly be anyone out there who would recognize her. She was so used to not using her magic now...perhaps she'd be just fine to stop using it. Perhaps she could fit in with the rest of the world.

Bea took a deep breath and glanced back at her cottage. The ramshackle house was just large enough for her to be comfortable, but not so large that she worried an intruder might be lurking in dark corners. The spell protected her from that, but everything looked different in the dark.

She was reminded forcefully of the knife that felt like a red-hot poker in her pocket. Bea had almost forgotten she'd slipped it into her cloak when she left the cottage, almost as if she'd planned to leave the moment she'd spotted it on the table.

There's a way back, she reminded herself. If she didn't like the world, she could always return.

***

Bea had walked for hours into the trees, her feet taking her far from the haven she'd created. She'd felt it dissolve as she left the boundary, shriveling up like a worm in the sun. Without her, the haven had no reason to exist.

So far, she didn't recognize her surroundings. She felt that to be a great comfort. She hadn't changed much in 200 years, but the forest had. Everything else had.

She'd left her haven just before dawn, when the sun hadn't even crossed the horizon, but now the sun crept higher, sending streams of bright sunlight through the tree cover above. As the ground began to slope upward and sweat covered her brow, she felt it—like her vision had doubled, just for a moment—she'd flashed back instead of forward, to when she'd stood here, in this exact spot...

She had seen this place before...hadn't she?

It was strange—the trees were familiar, their towering forms above her one of the only constants she had ever encountered. But there, ahead of her where the hill became steeper, were steps carved into the hillside: great logs of wood laid across them that she'd never seen before. There were also strange markings... words—no, letters—carved into some of the trees. Were they the markings of a path?

Or...had she encountered some kind of magic? She couldn't smell sulfur, but perhaps a masking spell—she stepped close to the nearest tree, her face inches from the rough bark as she tried to decipher the markings.

"Hello?"

She jumped, hand going to the pocket where her knife was concealed. She turned, slowly, towards the voice.

Below her, on a dirt path she'd only just noticed, stood a man.

He was tall and dark-skinned, with a strange red coat and large pack. From here, she couldn't tell the colour of his eyes, but she knew he was staring at her, his eyes round under the shadow of a dark cap.

"Do you need some help?" He started up the hill towards her before veering left so that he could leave the path. *How did he spot me from so far away?* She'd never seen these stairs before, so she'd watched them from a distance, but he had picked her out of the hillside before she could mask herself.

She had an inkling of where she was now, the thought making her still with anxiety. *People don't come to this part of the woods,* she thought, as he closed the distance between them. When he was five feet away, her limbs unfroze, and she stepped back.

"What do you want?" her voice was harsh with disuse.

He looked surprised, his eyebrows disappearing behind the cap. "I want to know if you need help. Are you lost? I could escort you out of the park."

"Park?" she echoed. "What park?"

The man's eyes widened; his steps slowed. He lowered himself, hands placating, and moved towards her more slowly. "This is Butter Pot Provincial Park. Miss, do you know where you are?"

Bea blinked at him, her hand still inside her cloak. The hilt of her knife was cold in her fingers. *What is a provincial park?*

"My name is Sam," he said. He was closing in on her now, she felt the squeeze of panic in her lungs. "I'd like to help you get home."

"Home." *That's right. I need to get home.*

She ran.

"Wait!" his voice echoed behind her, carrying up the hill before she outran it. Still, she heard his next words clear as a bell...clear as if she was standing on the same hill, 200 years ago: "Where are you going?"

The next part of his sentence was lost to the forest as she climbed, her legs aching. It'd been so long since she'd exercised like this; as her lungs expanded with the fresh air on the hill, she felt a laugh rise to her lips. The noise was hysterical and loud and cut off by a sob.

She missed this—running through the trees, being in nature... it was different in her bubble. The green wasn't as green, the air not as...fresh. It was too stagnant, too unmoving, too full of sulfur when she reached the boundary.

Behind her, footsteps on the wood told her she was being

followed. Icy fear struck her like lightning, straight from her crown to her soles. *If I can just reach the top*...she'd be safe. Back to her haven.

Her legs were so tired, her lungs filled with fire as each breath sawed in and out of her. She wanted to stop, but the heavy sound of boots on wood filled the silent forest like a death knell. *I'll be safe if I just –*

There.

She burst out of the tree line and scrambled for the edge, putting her back to it, just as she had 200 years ago, but this time, she wasn't surrounded.

Just one man, the one in the red coat, burst from the trees, his hands outstretched towards her. As he took her in, his eyes went wide with fear. He stopped short, taking careful, measured steps toward her like he was trying not to frighten her.

He didn't know what she could do; about the cliff. About her haven.

I have to get back...She took a step back to the edge, seeing the trees below, but feeling no fear. Not this time. The spell had worked before. It would work again.

"Stop, please!"

She shut her eyes against the familiarity of those words, spoken in an unfamiliar cadence. She couldn't stop. She needed to get home.

A few more steps back, and she could be there. The man was still a few feet away—he couldn't make it in time...she twisted her torso towards the drop and stepped out.

For one heart-stopping second, her foot fell into free space and she allowed herself a sigh of contentment—the words of the spell were on her lips, ready –

And then a large hand latched onto her wrist, wrenching her out of the air. His grip was too tight, his momentum too strong, sending her body flying back into his.

In a whirl of red and green, they tumbled down the hill, landing just before the treeline, tangled together in a pile of limbs. Bea's head hit the ground with a dull *thud* and the world around her went black.

***

She opened her eyes to the forest, her hands gripping feebly at the thin trunks of the densely packed trees. She struggled for traction, trying to use anything to help propel her up the hill as rain and mud squelched beneath her boots.

This was not her haven. But this was also not the cliff.

"Wait! Don't run, please."

That's Bo's voice... She knew it well, though she hadn't heard it in 200 years.

I can't stop. The words she'd thought so long ago thrummed through her body like wildfire, setting her legs alight with renewed energy. She was so tired, but she just couldn't stop.

Another old thought raced through her head: *I have to make it to the top.*

But what would happen if she simply stopped? This was the past—it had already happened. The trees couldn't protect her; she hadn't called on her haven yet.

Still, no matter her thoughts, her feet carried her forward, up the hill. Towards the place she'd first placed her boundary. It had been easier with the steps carved into the slope.

"Where are you going?" Bo's voice carried on the wind, up the slope, but it was accompanied by other voices. Men from the village, those who'd found out about her...Bo's pleas reached her too late. She was almost there. And then, she would be free.

But she was so tired. Bone-achingly so. She'd used too much of her magic, too much of herself, to keep her going...there was only strength for one more spell, and only if she reached the top –

She skidded to a stop, the mud nearly propelling her over the cliff. The hill she'd climbed so often with the other children had never seemed so high. Below her, the forest spread out in a rush of rain-soaked green. She could see the sea from here. If she tried hard enough, she might be able to hear the waves on the rock.

If not for the shouting.

She'd never used her magic for anything bad. *Never.* And yet, here she was. She stepped back, her heels on the jagged edge of the cliff. She'd fall into leaves and branches, likely break her neck and limbs before she hit the ground. If she hit the ground.

Raising her head, she watched as the first face came over the hill, then the next, and the next. She kept her hands fisted around her necklace, refusing to wipe the tears that streamed down her face. The worst part of all of this was that she recognized them. They were all older than her, bigger: Bo's father, his brothers and uncles and family friends. People who loved Bo.

People who used to love her.

And there was Bo, struggling to get through the burly mass of bodies. Even from here, she could see how pale he was, the sickly off-white of rotten milk.

"Bea, wait!"

He was always calling her. Calling her to slow down, to catch up, to wait for him...but now he was asking for one thing she couldn't do.

She could not stop.

She could *not* wait for him.

If she did, they'd both be dead.

Putting both heels over the edge of the cliff, she took in his face. He looked just like his brothers, only without their long beards and burly frames. Bo was still in the scrawny phases of adolescence...they both were.

Bea leaned back into the wind, letting it sweep her off the cliff as the men surrounding her fell away, replaced by the dark rock of the mountain.

Her words were ripped from her by the howling wind and she gripped her necklace tighter, the biting metal leaving indents in her palm. The smell of sulfur surrounded her like a cushion, comforting even in its atrocity.

Bo's face, the only pale spot in the dark sky above her, peeked over the cliff.

Then she fell through the trees and everything went black.

***

When she regained consciousness, it took a minute for her to open her eyes—something heavy lay across her torso, stopping her from taking a full breath. At least the squeezing around her wrist had stopped. He'd let go of her.

He.

She opened her eyes into round disks of deep brown just as he said, "What were you thinking?"

They'd landed with their legs tangled together, his torso across hers. His face hovered inches away, and she immediately sank back against the earth, pressing herself into the dirt.

He sat up quickly, extending a hand to help her. She ignored it, scooting back from him in the scrubby grass. A sharp pain radiated from her left elbow, just above where he had grabbed her.

"Did I..." at his side, his fingers twitched. He started to move towards her, but thought better of it, giving her space. "Did I hurt you?"

Bea nodded, not trusting her voice. The spell was on her lips, but it could easily be confused for other more dangerous spells. If she pronounced it wrong...worse, if she pronounced it right...*he'll go to my haven too.*

They sat there, staring at each other. She'd ripped his coat, but he didn't seem all that concerned about it. His eyes went from her face to her cloak, then to her shoes, which were worn and patched as best as she could manage. She'd never learned the spell for mending; she never thought it would be necessary. Though her haven had included a cache of spell books, they sat unused on her rickety shelves.

"You're dressed strangely." There was a hint of amusement in his voice. "What's your name?"

"You're the one wearing bright colours. What did you trade to get such a rich colour?"

His eyebrows shot up his forehead. His hat had slipped off in their tumble, revealing his shaved head. "What did I trade? Do you mean how much did it cost?"

"Yes."

"They gave it to me for training..." he looked puzzled. "Probably two hundred dollars?"

"Dollars? Did you not use pounds?" Now Bea was puzzled. She *had* been in her haven for a long time—200 years, she thought... had currency changed so much since then?

"I don't think we've used pounds since Canada got their own currency."

"Canada?"

"Miss, do you know what country you're in?"

Now she stared at him. He clearly thought she was insane. "Newfoundland, of course. What year is it?"

"1996."

No. There was no way that much time had passed. She glanced down the hill, towards the path with the wooden steps carved into it. The last time she'd run up the hill, there had been no steps. The last time, it had been 1736.

He must have sensed her preparing to bolt, because as she got to her feet, so did he.

"Where are you from?" He asked softly. The meaning was clear, though he looked nervous: *When are you from?*

"Please, let me go."

"I'm just trying to help," he said. At his shoulder, thunder crackled from a little box, the size of a letter. She hadn't noticed it before. Just then, a voice emerged from it, squawking, "Kane, what's your status?"

His left arm went for the box—a habit, she suspected—and as his eyes moved from hers to the box, she took off, scrambling back up the hill towards the edge.

She'd get back this time, she'd have to.

She didn't spare a glance behind her as she reached the edge and jumped—if she had, she might have seen Sam closing the distance between them.

She might have seen his hand close around the hem of her cloak, pulling him down towards his death.

If she'd seen him, though, would she still have spoken the spell?

The words left her lips, pronounced just right, and the smell of sulfur engulfed her once more.

***

Ironically, falling through the trees and into her haven felt a lot like falling through actual trees.

When Bea awoke, her limbs felt swollen and heavy, her neck stiff. She never thought she'd do this twice. It was a spell that one really only needed once.

She recognized the smell of the boundary before she opened her eyes. Dirt and muted freshness mixing with egg-like sulfur. Sunlight streamed in through the trees above her, searing her eyelids with golden light. It was just before noon and the sun was nearly right above her. She should move, go home –

A groan from nearby startled her eyes open. A few feet away, Sam lay in the grass, his left foot bent at an odd angle. Despite the pain in her elbow, Bea got to her feet and approached him carefully, as if he were a dangerous animal. When he didn't open his eyes at her approach, she stepped closer, the pain in her elbow growing more noticeable.

She watched the rise and fall of his chest from a distance, just to be sure, and then knelt beside him, careful to avoid his injured leg. He was a lot bigger than her—there was no way she'd be able to carry him...*but the books*...

Bea had no occasion to use the spell books that her haven provided—with it's help, she'd never gotten sick, and never injured herself besides paper cuts or nicks when she'd been careless in the kitchen. Now though, her books may actually come in handy.

She got to her feet, dizzy from her tumble on the cliff and falling into the haven—the first time she'd performed the spell, she'd been unconscious for hours, lying in the rain and mud. It still took a lot out of her, especially since she hadn't done any magic in the last 200 years. *No*, she corrected. *Almost 300.* Would she even have enough for another spell?

Bea started off down the well-worn dirt path, made from years of her feet traversing it. It was a miracle Sam hadn't broken his neck on the way down. The haven didn't make a cushion for him like it did for her—he had no magic it recognized.

As she entered the little cottage, she felt that something was different. The air was still and musty, as if she'd been gone for a few weeks instead of just a morning. Her bed, which sat in the corner opposite the small hearth, looked dusty. Where she stood, she could see the dust layered on her worn table, but as she turned on her heel, she felt goosebumps rise on her arms.

The bookshelves were empty.

Bea's fists unclenched as she rushed towards the shelves. Ignoring the ache in her elbow, her hands gathered dust as she swept them over every shelf, searching...

Come on...what had happened to the haven that provided her with everything? Had it turned on her because of Sam? Because she'd brought someone else inside?

She bent to the fireplace, fingers scraping over the stone as she searched blindly for some book, *any* book, to help her –

Her fingers bumped up against worn leather and she jumped back, startled. *Why is there a book in the stone?* Bea squinted in the dim light, sweeping her eyes across the stone as she searched for the book she'd missed. Her hands travelled down the rough rock face, searching every nook and cranny until her nail caught on something soft.

There.

Carefully, she wiggled the book free and settled on the hearth to examine it. With her nose nearly touching the page, Bea skimmed the blank pages, her heart in her throat. Sam wouldn't die from a broken ankle, but she couldn't get him out of the forest unless she fixed it...and if her haven had stopped providing for her...

The pages were mostly blank, but as she reached the last few, she recognized the wording of a spell, rhythmic and flowing, with twisty words that meant nothing. It was a spell for healing.

Bea blew out a breath and got to her feet. Her heart steadied in her chest, slowing until it was back to a normal pace. She leaned against the fireplace, letting her forehead rest on the cool stone. Her arm ached.

There's no way I can do both, she realized. Exhaustion was settling in, deep in her bones, and she knew that if she didn't keep moving, she'd stop for a long time. She needed food, and water, but with Sam to care for now...

She pushed off the fireplace and ran her right hand over the stone, the book clutched limply in her left. "Why are you doing this?" she murmured to the cottage. She imagined her words flowing through the stone, into the earth at her feet where it met the roots of the forest.

Bea held her breath, willing the beat of her heart to slow, just in case trees decided to answer her for the first time in over 200 years.

When the answer did come, it passed through her swiftly, like ripples on the water.

Because it's time to go.

***

When she made her way back to the clearing, tear stains wiped carefully from her cheeks, she was startled to see Sam sitting up. He was covered in sweat, his eyebrows scrunched together in pain. His eyes flitted around, taking in the unfamiliar trees—when they landed on Bea, they went wide. "Where are we?"

"This is my haven." She slowed her steps as she came closer, determined not to spook him. Bo had only seen her work a spell once, in a similar situation...if he reacted the way Bo had...

She tried to throw the thought from her mind. *The haven is no longer a haven,* she reminded herself. *And if he decides to leave, he'll have to find his way out of the forest first.* She still knew the forest well, despite the steps carved into the hill and his strange talking box. She could disappear with or without the haven's help.

Despite the fact that the trees had decided she wasn't welcome in the haven any longer, she could still feel their presence, too. They might help if he decided to attack her.

Still, she needn't worry about that. When she knelt beside him, he stayed still. There was no tightness in his body that suggested fear. In fact, though she hadn't seen another human in centuries, she recognized the expression on his face: relief.

"How is your ankle?"

"Painful," he ground out. "Definitely broken. I tried to splint it but with the angle it's at I don't think I can reach it."

"I can help if you'll let me."

Sam's eyes met hers and she noticed flecks of gold mixed in with the deep brown of his irises. "You're being very cool about all this."

"My mother and her sisters were healers. I saw a lot of things usually reserved for adult eyes. May I?"

Sam's chin dipped and she knelt by his foot, careful of her balance as she hovered above him. His toes were pointed almost entirely the wrong way.

"How old are you...?" He trailed off, and she realized he didn't know her name.

"Bea. I am over 200 years old, according to the year you've given me." She probed his twisted ankle with careful fingers, making sure to be as gentle as possible. Strangely, it felt nice to be of use to someone again after so many years.

"You look like you're in your twenties –" His words cut off in a yelp. Bea had twisted his foot so it faced forward once more. That was a trick she'd learned from watching her aunts at work. Her mother had been much gentler with patients, but often slower to ease their pain.

Bea laid the book on the ground, pressing the spine open so the pages lay flat. In the sunlight, she saw that the pages were yellow with age. The only spell in the book looked like it had been written ages ago, in thin, curvy lines that she was careful to sound out, lest she get it wrong.

"This will hurt."

Sam laughed. Or at least, he made a sound that echoed a laugh. "That's fine. I broke my arm once, during training, and that hurt much worse." She felt his eyes on her and wondered if he was looking at her arm. "Did you get hurt?"

"What were you training for?" she asked, placing both her hands on either side of his ankle bones. She could feel the fracture, how out of alignment the bones were. The pain in her elbow was nothing compared to what he must be feeling right now.

"To be a park ranger."

"Is that why you were so far out in the woods?"

"Yes. About six months ago I finished my training and now I patrol the trails and restricted areas." She felt his eyes on her as he said: "But that area with the steps, that's not exactly in the middle of nowhere. It's our most popular trail."

So if she hadn't run into him first, she may have met others. Would they have reacted the same way he did? "What does that mean—trail? Is it like a pilgrimage?"

"People travel to this forest and hike. They walk the paths and climb the steps to the peak. They take photos and videos and sometimes they get lost. That's where I come in."

Bea's chest felt suddenly concave. The haven must have been keeping people away from her for a long time...maybe it simply just...*got tired*. The thought made her stomach turn.

"Stay still." She pressed her hands to Sam's ankle. Ignoring his hiss of pain, she started to murmur the words of the spell, just under her breath so he wouldn't catch them. The smell of sulfur filled the air around them, thick and pungent.

Bea felt it as the bone knit back together, almost like an invisible hand had reached inside and sewn the jagged edges together. The moment the ankle was healed, her fingers began to ache. She pulled back as sweat dripped down her neck and back. She'd been right earlier—she wouldn't have enough in her for more spells today. Maybe not for a while, even. She was too out of practice, not used to flexing those muscles anymore.

She sat back on her heels and brought her gaze to Sam's. "All done."

"Is it...is it better?"

"Does it still hurt?"

"No," he mumbled. He pulled his leg up towards his chest, rolling his ankle and probing the bone. "Wow. Thank you," he smiled at her in a way that was familiar—the smile of those who she'd been able to help. She could see the questions in his eyes, but she was grateful he didn't ask. There were some things that were just too difficult to answer, and right at this moment she wasn't sure what she'd say.

Sam's eyes travelled down to her arm, which she cradled in her lap. She was exhausted, the pain growing worse now. "Let me see."

Bea held her arm out to him before she even thought about why that might be a bad idea. His touch was gentle, his skin warm, and he held her carefully, turning her arm over with expert hands.

"Are you a healer too?"

"Not exactly." He reached for the pack behind him and started to dig through its contents. "I had to take first aid and CPR, but I really only have the basics."

Before she could ask what 'CPR' was, he withdrew a roll of cloth from the bag. "Can I wrap it?"

Bea eyed the cloth, not sure it would help much, but she held her arm out obediently. He unrolled the cloth with quick fingers, wrapping it just tight enough from her upper arm to her wrist. The pressure helped, but the pain was still sharp. "I think it's just a sprain, but we should get you checked out by a doctor."

Bea didn't answer; her eyes went to the trees instead. High above her, the sunlight filtered down through the leaves; bright beams of light danced on the ground as the branches swayed. They'd told her very clearly she wasn't supposed to be here anymore. But as a gust of wind swept through the clearing, tangling Bea's hair and chilling her, she wondered, *what will I do outside?*

"This is your home, right?"

She peeked at him out of the corner of her eye. "It was. It's decided it won't be my home anymore."

"What do you mean?"

Bea bit her lip, running her fingers over the rough edges of the bandage. Would it be okay to explain it to him? He'd seen so much already, and so far he hadn't reacted poorly...still, in the back of her mind, she remembered the fear, the *horror*, in Bo's eyes when he saw her heal the Farron girl.

"If you don't want to tell me, that's fine," Sam said, his eyes on the scrubby grass beneath them. "But this is only the second strangest thing I've ever seen."

Well now, that was interesting. "The second?"

Sam's eyes met hers, and she had the overwhelming understanding that he was trying not to startle her. Warmth rushed through her at the kindness of the gesture. "I mean, this is the stranger of the two, but the first was more scary."

"Why?" He spoke as if falling through the sky and surviving was normal.

"When I was younger, the house I lived in backed onto the forest. There was a little creek back there I would fish and explore around. I wasn't supposed to go in too far, my mom would worry, but that never stopped me. That's how I met the Good People."

Bea went still at his words. There had been the talk of the hamlet she'd grown up in—superstition, really, but everyone on the island had story about the Good People—everyone was *terrified* of them.

She'd seen signs of them too; little flashes of movement here and there when she picking berries with her friends, small caps or snatches of cloth caught on branches too low for them to be human, but...

"What form were they?"

The corner of Sam's mouth quirked up, higher on one side. "They were lights—like will-o'-the-wisps in old stories. Just lights. I think was seven or eight; old enough to remember, at least. I followed them through the forest and got lost."

Bea noticed a sharp pain in her knees just then. Looking down, she saw she'd leaned towards Sam, so entranced by his words that her fingernails were biting hard into her skin. She relaxed her hands, pulling herself upright. "And?"

"And then it got very dark and my dad came out and found me. I was at least three hours into the woods by the time he got there."

"What was it like?" The words were out before she knew it— she'd always wanted to meet the Good People, talk to them maybe, but they'd largely ignored her. Her mother used it say it was because they disliked the smell of sulfur. Since the haven had been created, she'd seen not a one come her way.

"Terrifying." A strange look came over his face: a cross between peace and fear. He blinked, then shook his head. "And fascinating. I think there was some sort of song, or a melody I was following—it was so calm in the forest that day and I felt so at peace. But then when I heard my dad shouting for me and I finally turned around, it was pouring. I was drenched. Thank goodness I hadn't wandered too close to one of the cliffs."

"Yes." Her voice sounded far away to her ears. She'd heard of the trances that the Good People could put on someone—they were infamous for causing death most of the time...but perhaps that was why it was so easy for Sam to believe her. He was so far removed from her time, when people were terrified of the unknown, of her and her spells—but that was only part of it. He'd encountered something unknown, something otherworldly, and hadn't been afraid to go back into the forest.

He couldn't feel the trees, she knew that. But she had a feeling that he'd understand if she ever described it to him. They shared a common purpose, Sam and the trees. It was the reason he became a ranger in the first place: to protect those who were still lost.

Like rushing, a river travelling from deep underground and spreading up the trunks of the trees, Bea felt them then, spreading to the farthest branches and the highest leaves.

They gave her the answer to the question she hadn't even asked yet.

Could she trust him?

Yes.

Would he really help her?

Yes.

Sam got to his feet, rolling his newly healed ankle. She watched him as if from the end of a long tunnel as she slipped the pack over his shoulders and looked toward the boundary he couldn't see.

The sulfurous smell mixed with the scent of muted greenery, reminding her of safety, of comfort and protection and warmth. There was a reason the spell would only work in the forest—the trees held a special kind of power—protecting life inside their own boundaries, as far as their roots would reach.

Sam turned, his brow furrowed, head tilted to the side. Their eyes met, and he smiled softly. "Should we go? It's going to take some time to get back to the station."

He reached out to her with his left hand, his coat a blur of red in the sea of green.

She stared at his palm, rough with calluses, criss-crossed with lines that her aunt would have read like a book. A deep ache splintered through her heart.

Once, Sam had been lost. Once, Bea had been cornered. He ran and so did she, but the difference was this: he hadn't been afraid to go back to the thing that frightened him.

She looked up at the trees, craning her neck to soak in as much as she could. *I'll age now.* It was funny, she hadn't realized she'd made the decision until she thought that. But yes, year by year, at the same rate as the trees, she would change. Tear welled in her eyes, slipping hot and fast down her cheeks. She'd never be the same Bea, the same version of herself as she was right now...but the trees would change too.

As she'd made her decision, Sam had been silent. In front of her, his hand remained outstretched in silent invitation. Bea reached out and took his hand, offering a small smile. He helped her to her feet, careful of her elbow, and matched her pace as they started to make their way out of the forest.

At the boundary, she hesitated for only a moment at the invisible line, just long enough to feel the trees around her. Smiling with her, crying with her, *being* with her.

Then she stepped beyond the boundary and into the world.

The Beginning

Katrina Carruth

Katrina Carruth is a chaotic neutral writer, wife, and mother. She is obsessed with writing, cooking, horror, D&D, reading, coffee, rum, Nancy Drew games, tarot, and her delightfully weird family.

In the beginning, before the earth was *your* Earth and the heavens were *your* heavens, there was a garden.

It started with the first mother: a tree whose seed was gifted from the stars and penetrated Earth's virgin soil—splitting open in total darkness with no choice but to follow the light upward. The resilient sprout flourished into that which would birth all life.

Mother Tree's roots sank deep, all but kissing the core of her planet, and her limbs stretched out across the land and up toward the stars. She fought hard to prosper in the emptiness that was life with no other life, and her first years passed in the quiet sound of possibility.

Eventually, the cosmos blessed Mother Tree with an unexpected gift. Humble beings appeared before her, curious and silver-tongued, and introduced themselves as nameless gardeners, servants to her and cultivators of what they promised would be a fantastical garden.

They doted on Mother Tree, nourishing her with crisp, cool water and tending dutifully to the soil around her, preparing for what they knew was to come. Mother Tree did not think to question what might be expected of her, and the gardeners offered no explanation.

One day, Mother Tree found herself surrounded by the wide-eyed gardeners, beaming as they marveled at the newly sprouted buds speckled generously all over Mother Tree's miraculous self.

New growth meant new life: the dawn of the garden that would herald the world's precious beginning.

Cheers erupted around her.

"This is what you were created for!"

"...an honor to carry this weight of the world!"

"...everything is as it's supposed to be."

Mother Tree's glow matched that of the moon, illuminating the void that once consumed her isolated life. For weeks the gardeners watched Mother Tree in diligent shifts, coddling, comforting, and nearly smothering her. The gardeners' constant attention lifted Mother Tree's spirits as the weight of her children exhausted every fiber of her being, and the gardeners assured her that the worst would soon be over.

With love and the tenderest care, her buds bloomed. She dreamed of what they might grow into; imagined her days watching over them as they took on new shapes and weathered every season.

As each child matured, the gardeners waited in anticipation, whispering in hushed tones as the days passed. Though their behavior made Mother Tree anxious, she ignored her instincts and shoved her thoughts deep within her roots.

It wasn't long before Mother Tree felt her first child's hold weaken. Panic ensued as every gardener rushed to her side, fixated only on the young fruit and offering her no comfort. Mother Tree told herself this was for the best, that the well-being of her child should, and would always be, their top priority. Her trembling limbs shook the first ripe fruits free and the gardeners raced to catch them.

They praised her first birth with wild excitement as they whisked the children away from Mother Tree before she knew what was happening. Every attempt to protest was drowned by the sound of their celebration, and she was left alone to drown in the darkest sorrow.

As more fruit began to ripen, the gardeners lingered less frequently, and instead only visited her to pluck dropped fruit from the ground.

Eventually, they returned with seeds from her beautiful children and began planting them back into the soil. Mother Tree was too afraid to ask what they had done with the bodies—too afraid to believe the gardeners were not to be trusted.

Greed soon replaced awe as the gardeners became too impatient to let the world work in its own time. Mother Tree was helpless as they hacked her children from her body, spewing excuses about ripeness. They pretended not to hear the squeals and screams in their assault, but she heard every single one.

The gardeners smiled and built their fires, stopped hiding their actions in the shadows, and sang as they sharpened their blades. Mother Tree wanted nothing more than to crumble under the weight of her own branches. She had no place to hide, no power to stop them from maliciously ripping apart her children until their cries fell silent. She watched in agony as the gardeners charred their bodies directly over a sinful flame or dumped their chopped bodies into stews. Their teeth tore through their lifeless flesh, they laughed as juice dripped down their mangey jowls, and Mother Tree sobbed as they sang of their *success*.

Anguish consumed her as she understood all too late that creating life meant creating suffering and grief.

She pleaded with the gardeners but was met with scoffs. They suggested—no, insisted—that her purpose was one of sacrifice, that she was destined for this and only this and should be happy with her role in creation.

Mother Tree asked who decided this for her but, again, received no fair response.

Her hope disappeared and took her energy and strength with it. As the unbearable agony continued, new buds failed to blossom on Mother Tree. Her roots thinned and rotted, and her figure hunched into a disheveled curve. The gardeners quickly started using words like "ungrateful" and "lazy" and demanded that she "get it together." It was easier for those not expected to create life to believe it should be enough.

Mother Tree felt heavier each day, unsure how they expected her to grow when she wasn't allowed to hope for something better.

Touting the need to preserve their own energy and stop wasting it on Mother Tree, the gardeners took it upon themselves to absolve her of her duties.

Wide smirks glistened as they approached with shimmering axes. They told her not to worry, that they would still find a way to make use of her—one where she'd remain frigid, voiceless, and immobile. A gardener, now woodsman, marched mercilessly to her foundation and swung violently at her belly. He stepped back after each *whack* to admire his work as her layers weakened and the gash in her trunk grew. Her spirit diminished one sliver at a time, and after what felt like an eternity, Mother Tree fell to the ground, limp and lifeless.

Reduced to a stump, Mother Tree's severed remains were tossed into the fire to warm the gardeners sitting comfortably around it. Her children watched in horror, fearful of the day they, too, would be reduced to nothing.

This Sweet and Bitter Fruit or, Ladon's Lament

Maeghan Klinker

Maeghan is a postgraduate student studying Medieval English at the University of St Andrews where she spends her time reading old books and brushing the dust off of stories. When she's not stumbling over medieval texts, she spends her time reading sci-fi and fantasy books in Modern English, writing stories, talking to the trees, and going on walks with her dog. Confronted with infinite knowledge and only one question that can be answered, she would like to know: if the universe is expanding, what is it expanding into?

Not once upon a time or long ago, but between this breath and the next, a Tree grows from the earth. No matter how sharp the blade, it cannot be felled. Unlike most of its kind, it wanders restless as a thing uprooted. It shifts like a seed on the wind until it comes upon an apple tree or a pomegranate or an almond, and for a season, the Tree settles into its roots.

You will know the Tree has come by the golden shimmer of its fruit. One day it grows ripe and ordinary, the next it winks with Midas-touched hues. It is a subtle difference. A shift of the light, a glimmer caught at the flickering edge of sight that turns your head. It is tempting to run your fingers over the skin, just to assure yourself of the difference. Even easier to pluck it from the branch and bring it to your eye and then your lips. From there, it is nothing to peel-crack-bite the skin. No matter the tree—fig, date, peach—the fruit is both sweet and bitter. Those who taste it say it lingers on the tongue.

For some, it is worth it. Everyone knows what the Tree can give. Few think to ask what it takes.

I have heard the stories sung during the harvest as the scythes reap the ripened grain and whispered around the hearth during the longest and darkest nights. I have heard them spoken from the pulpit laced with brimstone and fire and told in lulling voices to coax children to sleep. Across every land and over every sea, the stories have bloomed in weathered voices and reverent whispers, persistent as a weed. Doubtless, you have heard them.

Everyone who speaks of the Tree knows it is abundant with gifts: knowledge, power, bounty. It is a fulfiller of wishes. Some say only the kind and virtuous can find the Tree, or that the Tree only bestows its gifts upon the worthy. They are wrong. I have tasted of the Tree's fruit, once, and I am neither kind nor virtuous. My wish was far from worthy. But I paid the price. I have given what the Tree takes.

I tell you this as a warning: the Tree is a hungry thing, and it will exact its price from anyone willing to taste its fruit.

You seek it, do you not? I recognize that look in your eye: a sharpness like hunger, a madness like hope. Do not try to deny it. You must have sought long and far to end up here. Take comfort, little one, you are close.

No, I will not tell you the way. You are a fool to be here at all. Thousands of years I have roamed this earth, guarding the Tree, waiting for it to die. But the Tree cannot be felled. It does not wither. Its roots twine through the cracks of this world, pushing it apart, holding it together. It is an endless and terrible embrace.

I have followed the Tree from Aidenn, and Eamhna, and the Garden of the Hesperides. I have chased its sweetness on the air across every land above the waves and several that have long sunk beneath them. Its bitterness is as familiar to me as the warmth of the sun on my scales. I have seen its glimmer come upon the Juniper tree sequestered in its mountain hold and the towering fronds of the Date palm rooted in the desert sands. Long have I guarded the Tree, trying to dissuade those fools like you who seek it, but the whispers of the Tree are insidious, and there are always those eager to listen.

Do you hear its voice on the wind? How far the words carry. Its whispers pass from treetop to treetop, dance unseen from root tip to root tip, until it blooms like a fungus at the rotting heartwood. Such sweet lies lay in its susurrate words. Such awful truths.

You have come to the Tree looking for salvation. I tell you now to turn away: the Tree gives no blessings. It grows only curses.

You call me a liar? Well, you are not the first. I have been named Serpent, Ladon, Wyrm-of-the-Fruit. I have been cursed and reviled by those who took without thinking of the cost. But it is up to you: either I lie, or the Tree does, and I grant no wishes. For many, it is an easy choice.

Do you hesitate? You have journeyed far. Your clothes are ragged and torn, the sandals at your feet bloodied from the miles beneath them worn into your skin. You have come seeking a miracle. I can taste the smell of your desperation on my tongue. And yet, you hesitate. Could it be that you believe me? You would be the first.

Go on, ask. I know that you are curious.

I was young, like you, when I came upon the Tree. The whole world was young and had not yet settled into its shape. Being was malleable, and I was as often legged and winged as I was scaled and slithering. I was as shifting as the winds, though less free. I yearned to see the world, changeable and unsettled as it was, each day filled with wonders made and unmade beyond my reach.

It was then that the shimmer of the golden curse came upon a plum tree in my mother's garden. I was tempted by the sweet offerings of its fruit. Not once did I think of the glimmering, bitter skin it was wrapped in.

And my wish was granted. I have seen every hidden crevice of this world, every marvel, in my pursuit of the Tree. I have seen fires burn on the ocean and the flicker of colors beyond name slither through the sky. I have witnessed great nations rise and fall. I have marveled at beasts unseen by human eyes. I have traveled to islands born of mist that disappeared with the sun and basked upon the peaks of mountains that pierced the sky. I have tasted infinity poured from a thimble and heard the singing of an endless expanse of ice, and not once have I been satisfied.

This, you must understand: the Tree is grown of wanting. It feeds on the world's desires, on the endless ache, on the unquenchable need. It cannot be sated, and neither can those who taste its fruit. Once your teeth have pierced the skin, the juice slaked your stated thirst and your wish been fulfilled, the taste will linger on your tongue. I taste it still.

To eat the fruit of the Tree is to never be content again. A cavern grows in your chest. A hollowness is carved in your belly. It does not matter how you try to fill them. The Seed has already taken root. You will always be wanting.

Oh, but the Tree is clever, it knows what is easiest to take. Some never even notice the taking.

Ah, you think it is not so high a price. I see your doubting eyes. Go on then. Mind the gnarled roots and grasping thorns. Find it, if you can. You will not mind if I coil my way through the branches alongside you. It has been a long time since anyone has wandered this close, and the Tree is bitter company. It does me good to hear another voice unshaped by leaves.

Besides, I have sworn to see this through.

***

You are a persistent little thing. No, I will not give you a hint. Were you not listening? I am neither kind nor virtuous, or did you think that too was a lie? No, I will not aid you in this folly. You must stumble upon it like all the rest. The brambles are exacting their due, though, aren't they? Your legs are a bloodied mess. You must be weary. There is a stream not far from here that flows fast and cool. I could show you that, at least. Surely it would be better to breathe a moment and think. There is no saying whether you will discover what you seek. You might pass by the treasured limb like a moth upon rough bark, like a Tree hidden in a forest. Such things are easy to miss.

No? Well, you cannot fault me for trying. It is all that keeps me from going mad. Or perhaps it is a kind of madness that drives me to this fruitless task. I admit, it is a sort of vengeance that I seek. The last thing on this earth that might bring me any shiver of satisfaction is to thwart the Tree. But it is a conniving thing. The more I want, the stronger the Tree grows, and I want so terribly. No wanderer has yet believed me. You yourself remain unconvinced, though I think I might dissuade you still. You have a canny way about you —

Alas, your eyes are sharp.

I had hoped—but never mind. Behold, the treasure you have sought. It is both grand and terrible, no? Smaller than you thought? Well, it is often the way of such things. The Tree is, after all, only a tree. I believe this one is called a medlar tree. It is a peculiar fruit; strangely shaped and oddly eaten. They say it is best harvested overripe, nearly rotted on the branch. An apt choice, with the Tree's gleam upon it. I remember well its taste. You will know it soon enough.

Wait a moment, child. Wait. There can be no hurry now. The Tree will not up and leave. Not when you are so close. Sit a while. Rest your feet. The roots are as good a place as any. See how they knot together? It will make a fine seat. Come now, there is no need for reverence. You will give what the Tree takes soon enough; it can stand to bear your weight for a moment.

There, unlace your sandals. Feel the earth beneath your toes. You have chosen a beautiful day for damnation. I am not sure a softer breeze has ever blown. Take a deep breath. Savor the sweetness on the air. You must be pleased. You have found what you long sought. Revel in this moment: you have accomplished what many could not.

There could be contentment here if you were willing to claim it. But I see how your hungry eyes wander, straying towards the gilded fruit. I do not miss how your fingers twitch towards the branch. Well, I cannot stop you. Pluck the bitter fruit, if you will. Look, the Tree is making it easy for you. The heavy golden boughs lean down magnanimously. Your wish is well within your reach.

Ah, you feel it, don't you? The shiver that passes through the world as your fingers graze the leaves. Fate holding its breath. Patience, child, one moment more before you pull it from the branch. Peer deeply into the gilt curse's sheen. Do you see the shadows? Reflections, surely, you will argue, but see how they flicker? Go on, look closer. Do you see it now? Yes, I see that you do. Your complexion is quite ashen. Your hands shake, your fingers tremble like the aspen.

Yes, little one. Pull back your hand. That's it. Not many have seen the specters of the fruit. Not many are willing to look. They were seekers once, like you. They were filled with such awful wanting. It consumed them, like a rot from within, as the Seed took root. Perhaps one day I will join them. Perhaps you.

That's it. Take another step back. Another. Ah, you cannot help but see them now. The twisted faces, the hollow eyes. Such wide and gaping mouths. It is a savage want that gnaws on them like hunger. They would tear apart this world to slake their desires. They are the Tree now. Will you join them?

At last. At last. You remember the way? Yes, turn your back on this place. Even now, the gleam begins to fade. This feeling—I had nearly forgot—ah, but the Tree is clever. I had thought just a taste, to turn away just one, would be enough. I should have known better. I have tasted of this sweet and bitter fruit, and I shall always be wanting. But look! A single leaf fallen, curled and brown. In all my long years hounding the Tree, I have never yet seen such a sight. No matter how sharp the blade, the Tree cannot be felled. But perhaps... if enough of those who sought it turned away... it might one day wither.

Oh, but I am an ancient fool, and you are wise beyond your mortal years. There is no sweetness for you here; I can offer you no wish. Take my blessing as bitter recompense.

Go now and walk gently, child, for the leaves are listening and the Tree whispers ravenously beneath our feet.

Step softly, little one, its roots go deep.

Hunger

Meg Malone

I'm Meg Malone, a speculative fiction
writer currently based in Milwaukee,
Wisconsin. I earned my B. A. from
Illinois State University in 2011,
specializing in Anglo-Saxon and
Arthurian Literature. I taught college
writing for nearly a decade in Illinois,
Iowa, and California, while also working
as a copywriter. In 2021, I decided to
refocus my career on fiction writing,
reimagining spaces for women to lead,
to be victorious, independent, and
unapologetic. Rooted in curiosity and
hope, my writing explores survival,
nature, and the bonds we forge at the
fringes of reality.

We do not mourn the dead. The dead go with the trees. They burrow into the whorls and climb up the vein-vines, and they live on where the roots go deep.

For centuries, we held our vigils at the base of the woods where the trees congregate against the border, against the water, against our bodies. Then came hallowed earth and the masons and the long, long memory of stone, and with it went the rawness and the tales and the short, short devotion to the human in nature.

Distance grew between the forest and the concrete, and the forest lost its realness and people started to mourn without really knowing what it was they mourned for.

But this is not us. Here, at the edge of the world, we cannot forget the trees if we tried.

My family takes the dead to the trees and feeds the trees and feeds the hungry souls stuck to the slick insides of bones. They feed each other, in the end, and they barely need us at all.

I do not know if we are human or not. It never occurred to me to ask for proof. The town asked. I did not. My family did not. We do not. We live on the border of the trees and the town, human enough. Close enough, our skin course and grained, like the neck of a tree. We eat and we sleep and we breed, and when the sun goes down at the end of the year, we die like the rest.

So who cares what I am. I do not care. My name is Maren. My name did not come from the forest, but came on the lips of a hurricane. It might mean the sea and it might mean war. Since it is not ours, we can never say for sure. It bothered me once, on the night the river dried, but I do not let it bother me now.

What matters is that I am Maren and my hands go to bodies and the bodies go to trees who ask me nicely what unused voices and empty skins and pretty colored orb-eyes I bring them today. There are no tears and there is no sadness and when the young woman hugs the old tree, she feels her grandfather's arms in the branches nudging her elbow. He talks to her and in wood-groans and chemical signals, he tells her to be a good girl and love her mother better and never ever stop knowing that there is a hunger that lives in trees that lives in us, too.

The grey wolf, small for his size, comes and sits at my feet. "You are far away today."

I pat his thick-furred head and listen to the salivation warming up his teeth, but I keep petting, because we have an agreement. "There are many bodies and less trees, and yet my trees are starving. I feel sadness in the clouds that the trees picked up from the ground and showed around to the sky, and I cannot stop wondering what to do. There is no clear, good thing to do."

A mighty pine leans her knees in close to us, her cloud hatted head tilting so her eyes might see us a little better.

"A hunter comes our way," she says. "A tall boy on tall legs."

I squat down and put my nose to the wolf's nose. "What would you do, wolf?"

He cocks his head and flicks one ear. "I would eat."

Except when the trees start to starve, there is no short path to eating. Their hunger grows deep and continues to grow deep. It will gnaw at the foundation of the planet and chew up the core and toss heat into the air in an eagerness to satiate that grinding hunger.

Then there is me at the bottom of generations. From grandmothers to mothers to daughters, my family has fed the trees. Now I am alone and small. And my hands, with their strong joints and talon nails for gripping skin and thin and brittle bones, return to the trees continuously empty.

I stretch out my hands across my ropy thighs and I listen to the moans of the trees in my vicinity. The mushroom caps puff up their lips and exhale and I feel their frustration with the long life of trees and the short life of rot.

A slender strand of drool crawls down the wolf's jowls. "I will eat and the trees can eat me."

I click my tongue and shake my head. "You eat the people and the people will beat you. They will beat you and your den and the trees that shelter you. You know the agreement. We do not break the agreement."

An oak drops a branch on the wolf's head and berates him with a stern rustling of leaves.

"We do not break the agreement," the wolf concedes, shaking spittle free. He watches me and I watch the hunter.

My stomach grumbles and I sink my hips into the mossy peat beneath me. I want to cross my arms and pout, to jut out my lip and let tears slip like raindrops down my neck. To act and feel like a child does when hunger pulls at the pink membranes of the stomach and difficulties patter from the sky faster than one can catch them. But I am grown up and that is no way for a grown up to act.

The hunter steps deeper into the forest and the wolf tenses at my side. The trees arch their backs and crane their heads.

I leap to my feet and the wolf leaps up with me. A snarl escapes his mouth. "I would eat," the wolf says again. I feel his hunger rubbing against my bones. Surrounding me, the hunger inside the trees does the same.

"The hunter has a right of passage," I remind them. So long as he, too, follows the agreement. I wonder what would happen if he does not. Arboreal hunger presses into my sides and the wolf sniffs at the taste of my skin. I question if the clear, good thing to do is right in front of me, walking my way. I know well, though, that if I break my agreement, the wolf will break his. One stone will fall into the next.

The wolf goes his way and the mighty pine straightens her boughs. I am left on my own. I feel the hunter's footsteps as he creeps across the ground, each vibration rubbing the soles of my feet. My skin shudders as he exhales and my bones rumble as he jumps down a ravine, booted feet striking the bottom.

It is not simple, this temptation to feed my trees, but there is no denying its clarity.

This hunter wanders here, into my part of the woods. How does he not feel the starvation in the trees, how they lean and lick at the thin strip of skin between his collar and his neck? His soul echoes inside his lungs and the forest roars with hunger.

I cannot blame them for what they want and what they need.

There are so many trees and so few bodies to bring and only me left to do what many more did before, together.

I stalk through the underbrush, feet padding, quiet and familiar and steady. The hunter stumbles over a root and I hear a young aspen snicker.

"Knock his head, he might. Fall into my mouth, he might," the aspen sing-songs.

I toss the aspen a glare and the groans and clacks fall silent and still. But I feel what they need and what they want and, once again, I cannot blame them.

Clouds skate low and brush the heads of elders. A squirrel burrows into the peat, two hops south of an elm, three strides east of an alder and the nut is gobbled into an open mouth and the gut goes quiet.

I am now in the path of the hunter. He studies the ground with long, lithe fingers and his neck bows like a leather strap as he observes what he sees. I linger between two twin trees, linked at the hip, a shadow there and not.

It was not long ago that people stayed at the borders and waited their turn, waited till their hearts stopped and the forest welcomed them in.

Back then, people did not cry over the dead. They looked at the forest and they saw where time ceased to move. They watched the sun chase the moon in the sky and the stars trip into the earth and the earth gobble them up, and in these motions, the people felt where they fell in a bigger rotation.

All things rotate, around each other, around routine, around bodies, heavenly and full of flesh. It is not the ticking passage of the clock, but the natural movement of a snake sinking teeth into her own tail.

It was back then, not long ago, that we agreed to coexist, the forest keeping spirits and the people keeping the forest. How long, I wonder, does it take to forget?

The memory of food is short, fullness fleeting as rabbits. We cup our memories like soft caterpillars in the night, but they rarely keep still. As sleep takes us, the memories crawl back down our ears and slide down our necks and drop with spiny feet onto the hardwood floor. They run away. They find their path into the forest.

The earth keeps moving and when the bodies do not make it to the trees, we feel ancestors trapped inside our chests. Watching this hunter thud and stomp his way across our bark-bones, it makes my heart earthquake. I become dense and heavy and full of sadness, because already he does not remember who came before and where they went or why any of this matters.

He slices the tender flesh of his hand on a thorn and a unanimous wail erupts from the starving trees.

There are times when I wake up and feel the universe spinning inside my chest. It is so real, I might peel back my ribcage, one curved bone at a time, and watch the stars and nebulas and galaxies tumble out, the moons to follow. Souls that are not eaten by the trees, I imagine them in my chest with the moons.

The hunter jabs his foot into a sapling, into brush. He tears himself a path and he cuts into the softness of the woods until it allows him to pass. He forces his intent and we have no strength but to yield.

"For now," I whisper to my own ear as around me the trees cry and their stomachs groan in the earth and the mushrooms pout.

I feel loneliness come upon me like splinters and the lonely weight of an impossible feat.

From between my twin trees, I slip free and, putting hand before hand and foot before foot, I crawl down the hillside. Silence folds around my shoulders and the little living things in the mud pull the sounds I make into the earth where they swallow them up. The mushrooms snicker as I pass and the snaking vines follow me with waxy, curious eyes.

They witness our agreement written on our cells and they witness me and the disintegrating boundaries that exist between the thing that should be done and the thing that needs to be done. Flakes of resolve flit like amber dust through my pores and fall onto tree-tongues.

They do not have to ask why I move closer to the hunter. They do not ask why I might break and why I might shatter and why I might destroy myself. They do not ask, because they are hungry. Because we've been shrinking from the world and losing our power and increasingly we've been forgotten, overwritten by what appears shiny and new and full of better worth.

They do not ask, because trees do not have mouths. They have roots and porous under-earth and they breathe and they speak in chemicals that touch the skin and touch the soul and sink in deep where the unconscious can hear the words they spill.

The hunter cannot hear how silent the trees have fallen. No chatter, no gossip, no stories. They are watching me and they are watching him and they are watching the distance shrink between us.

I once believed, when I was a small girl, that if I could peel back my ribs, one by one, and watch the moons trip out of my body,

I might know that stardust lingers in our skin. I might hear stars the way I hear trees and I might fall away into the sky when I have no body left to hold me.

I wondered if I would see my ancestors tumble out with my blood and all that star-matter. They would tell me secrets and tell me how they kept the trees fed and tell me where the bodies go after the trees are sated. They would tell me how I did not fail them after all.

Like the river that crushed its banks, my ancestors would flow between their death rage and their history and their connection to me and we would understand each other. I would not be shamed and I would be free.

My ribs, though, would not peel. I was never allowed to see what sparkled inside my veins, what burned infinitely and far away and right up close where all things are when we miss them most. No family tapped me on the shoulder with a hand like my own and tilted my chin up to a face with more angles than mine and said those words I needed to hear.

That I am forgiven and that I did not eat the river in vain.

I crouch on my heels as the hunter comes to the base of the hill. He is lean and tan across the back of the neck. The corners of his brown eyes crinkle into butterfly wings and I wonder if any children followed him today.

In the town, there are people with his forehead and a nose gone lumpy with age. Bright eyes with a splash of blue with frames just the same and lashes that sweep up, dramatic and dark. When they lay the table, five matching hands in a spectrum of old to young set their palms against the grains of wood.

In the town, they say this matters and that we should care that people are big. People are traceable above ground and in their blood and on the insides of bones. They possess surnames and faces and hands that are distinctly human, but they still map their lineages in terms of trees and we are not meant to notice that.

My feet and hands go still. The voice of my grandmother ripples over my eardrums and up the ragged bark of the oldest trees that ate her. *We feed the forest. We feed ourselves through their need of us. There is no higher purpose for people such as us. One bite at a time, we will bring green into this world again.*

Bring green, she said. Bring the world back to life. In the forest, everything rotates. Life turns to death turns to food turns to compost turns to seeds turns to life. Turn for turn, we all return to the beginning of the loop.

The ground settles beneath my toes and I spot the flourish of mushrooms with their soft caps and my gaze turns up to the big oak beside me. Her branches sag towards the dirt and they are bare. Only a few wispy leaves cling to the top of her bowing head. She is tired and old and ancient. Ancient as the sun and the mountains and the first stars that struck a lonely rock in a lonely vast darkness.

My grandmother's skin ripples between the deep grooves of bark and when I settle my finger between the thick tracts, her chest rises and falls and rises and falls. Her heartbeat shudders through dense rings and travels up my bones and I feel her, feel her inside my skin and inside my ribs and inside the twisting, curving path of my gut.

My family, they were so angry when they died. Rage ran endless, and then there was only me. Across the shallow valley, the wolf watches me. His face is hollow and his knife-teeth beam.

We are all hungry.

The hunter gets closer. He thinks he doesn't make a sound, but we all know he's here. We know the distance between his limbs and every tree in the forest. We know the distance between him and me.

He is hunting the wolf and I am hunting him and out of habit, the wolf is hunting me.

The trees click their tongues at me and the elders utter low ho-hums as they watch my hands and they watch my feet grip and release the ground. They murmur my name across the peaks and the valleys and the thin, serpentine waters that cut the forest in two and across the one river husk with its dried out mud and dried out bones.

There is an order that exists inside and above the ground. It starts down low, in close to the granules and the crawling, inching things below the dirt. Slow spirals define it, arcs passing close enough nearly to touch. Only by turning the spiral on its side and climbing in close enough for the nose to hover can we see that space exists between the turns.

In slow spirals, this order reaches from the rocks and into the sky. It might go beyond and through the moon, but we've only learned to see it this far, to the edge of the atmosphere where air becomes an egg shell against the mothering dark.

It is forest order. Nature order. Balance and symbiosis, mutual progression and mutual regression. If the trees thrive, we thrive. If the trees starve, we starve.

The trees tell stories of forests that are only knee high and forests that are under water. Some, they say, are too small for the eye to see. But the order is there in all of them.

The hunter has a right to pass through the forest, just as a vine has a right to choke an alder and a sapling may break concrete. The hunter may crush small plants beneath his boots and take the flesh of trees. He may take what he finds and tear it away from the sinew it belongs to. He may clutch his booty to his breast and feel victory for his violence. He may return home and share that which leaves the forest bleeding.

I know this. I know it as deeply as I know the contours of my own hands, the taste of my mouth upon waking up, and today I lose the sense of it. Where is our retaliation? When is the taken replaced, the damage healed? I hear the answer the way my grandmother taught it to me, her fingers tracing soft circles against my scalp.

She told me that we are not defined by the brutality of men. We are the women who keep the forest fed on the bodies of the dead. The dead live on in the trees and the trees live on around us and the living do not mourn the dead.

This is the reason, I realized as I got older, that I could not peel back my ribs and see the universe spill out over my fingers. What is consumed is already changed. It is part of the order of things, part of the rotation, part of the cycle where the snake bites her tail.

The wolf crouches low, his yellow eyes blinking in my direction, like we are two ends of a scale. I do not need eyes to tell me the closeness of the hunter. In every direction for a mile, the forest is lit up with micro-movements and sounds, with the rain of small atoms leaving and entering through pores.

I am right in the hunter's path and still he does not see me.

I do not know if I am human or not. I do not know if that matters or not. All I feel is hunger. The trees, the wolf, my own. Today, I feel threads shredding.

A long time ago, I was a fool who pulled a storm in from the sea and flooded the river. Mothers and grandmothers and daughters, I washed my family away, and I cannot reach them. I drank the river dry and still I cannot reach them.

We abide by the agreement, by the slow spiral of nature. We feed the dead to the trees and inside our bodies, the universe burns, and around us the trees go hungry and the wolves go hungry and the mushrooms go hungry and the town goes hungry. We are all hungry.

We are all here, in the path of the hunter. We are where no one sees us.

I do not know if I am waiting or watching. I do not know if I am readying or staying still. Across the shallow valley, the wolf sits down on his haunches. He cocks his head at me and again I hear him say, "I would eat."

I would eat, too, if it were even possible to feed my hunger, this hollowness left behind by a hurricane.

The earth rises towards my fingertips. Tension hums in the trees. We do not want to break. We do not want to shatter. My family would never have considered it, but my family is not here. My family is not me and they are not faced with a forest without bodies to eat. What was handed between grandmothers and mothers and daughters and me broke before I even got here.

With this one hunter, a river would flow. Those with hands and noses like his would follow, searching and shouting and wondering. We would eat them, too. More would come, first to find answers, and then in vengeance. We would eat them, too.

We starve, because the world has forgotten the trees, but here—here we cannot forget the trees if we tried. The trees consume us and the trees become us and we hear our family names darting through their pores. We come here, again and again, to find the familiar faces and angles and voices that we lost.

We do not mourn, because we know they are here. We only need to lean in close enough, near enough to bark, to hear them and feel them, to hold them and have them hold us in return.

In the end, we ask whose agreement it was and what hold did it have over the sanctity of our lives. In the end, we wonder what might have changed, if we'd been free from the start. If a tree could be a tree and the wolf, a wolf. If I could be from the sea and the women before me could be lupins and birds and shimmering insects. If we could be as we were meant to be. If we could be where things grow and there was no hunger.

I claw at my ribcage and I squeeze my eyes shut. Even if I cannot make it open, I can imagine it opens, my ribs, with a small latch at the center of the breastbone. No moons or suns or congregation of planets tumble out. Instead, I imagine them nestled in the soft flesh of my lungs and my heart. They orbit, undisturbed by my interruption, through the many openings my organs provide.

Here, we do not mourn the dead. The dead go with the trees. They burrow into the whorls and climb up the vein-vines, and they live on where the roots go deep and where the leaves watch the stars shine.

I close my ribcage and I put my nose to the wolf's, who now stands at the end of my toes. We breathe in and out and in and out, the two sides of a scale.

The hunter does not even see me.

Break Fresh Ground

Callie S. Blackstone

Callie S. Blackstone writes both
poetry and prose. Her debut chapbook
sing eternal is available through
Bottlecap Press. Her online home is
calliesblackstone.com.

I inherited many things with her house: sweaters organized by color, a set of teacups whose pattern I knew by heart, the two apple trees out back.

On the first night I moved into the house I warmed my hands by making some tea. She grew and dried the mint herself. I looked out the kitchen window into the darkness. There was no moon and the only lights were the masses of white apple blossoms staring back at me from the dark.

My thoughts about them were simple back then: I could make apple pies or butters. I could run a little cottage industry; I could wear one of her aprons and sing her songs quietly over my concoctions. I would bring a little money in from the local bed and breakfasts, but it wouldn't be about that. It would be about keeping her memory alive. I would call it Sadie's Sweets, or something saccharine. I would take aesthetically pleasing photos and post them on Instagram. Local guests would ask their hosts where the apple scones came from and the answer would be me, me, me–and Granny.

I knew those dreams would likely die down when I actually researched what it would take to start a business. All I would probably do is wander out to the yard and pick fruit from the branches; I would lounge under them and eat until my hands ran wet with the juices.

As I began to settle into her home, I created my own nightly routine. And despite my name being in her will and on the deed, the place always belonged to her. After I got home, I struggled to determine what dinner to make for one; I would eat while watching something bland on TV, just so I wouldn't feel alone; I would go into the kitchen and make mint tea from one of the plants she had grown over the years.

I initially relied on mint tea because the plant is so prolific. It would take forever for me to drink all of it. I had begun maintaining her garden and lawns; she let a patch of mint grow wildly in the back, away from the garden, and I knew mint would be there for the rest of time even if I wanted to trim it or cut it away. There were always new shoots and the scent hung in the air. It was safe to drink the mint, it would never run out. *Mint for healing,* she used to say. *Mint for a fresh start.*

The tea, the home—all a fresh start. It was all a fresh start and I knew that was what she would have wanted.

She had ruled the pantry and was strict about it. She was the only one who was permitted entrance. I had to allow myself in slowly, despite my name on the deed now. First, I spent days placing my hand on the doorknob. Then, cracking the door in degrees that got larger and larger. Then one step over the threshold. Then another.

Then the wall of scent of some spice hit my face and held me frozen amongst the jars. It was there that I first cried for her, the closet cradling me as her arms had done while she was alive. I fell to the ground and did not explore the pantry further that night.

I was eventually able to stand in front of the rows of jars with her scratchy, almost illegible handwriting on the labels. I recognized most of the herbs by sight. Despite not allowing me in the pantry, she had passed down knowledge about herbs and what our people had used them for. She often kept a few jars handy on the kitchen counter, easy and accessible–mint, dandelion, burdock, bilberry, nettle.

As I gained courage, I looked at a few jars every night. I still wasn't brave enough to open any of them. I suspected they would remain pristine like a museum exhibit until it was my own time to leave the house. Sure, she had taught me how to foster the plants myself, and I could–I had inherited her green thumb–but these were plants she had poured her own energy into, that she had hung in the basement to dry, that she had jarred and labeled. Besides the mint, a crazy plant that will never die, it didn't feel right to drink any of the teas stored there. It didn't feel right to use up these finite resources she left behind.

But I still let myself enter the pantry and look. I still inhaled that mysterious spicy scent that I had come to associate with her. When I stepped over the threshold each night I murmured "Granny" and it was like making an offering to her. I always wondered if she could hear me.

Another night, another herb, another recited remedy. I was surprised by how many of them I knew and how much I knew.

That was until I got to an unknown section of the closet.

These jars did not carry the names of herbs. In fact, I was not sure what the words on them said. Her handwriting was scratchy; sometimes I could see where her old fingers began to fail and the letters drifted off.

This was interesting.

Sadie was a woman of contradictions. While I had grown up she had always been honest. She never hid anything from me. My childhood was lined with my grandmother's stories about growing up as the child of Irish immigrants who fled the famine, about all of her herbal knowledge; yet there was always a sense of power that hung around her that I could never understand.

That was my granny: a supernatural force, always there when you needed her, always there with her big laughter and something to make you feel better–whether that was tea or cookies.

But what mysterious remedies was she offering in those jars?

I stood in the dimness of the room and stared into the first jar marked with the illegible word for a long time until the white chalked label seemed to glow back at me. I focused on each letter over and over until it lost its form and meaning. In this state I was slowly able to make them out, the point and legs of an A, the sharp angles of the M. The label read ALARM.

An ALARM? Like on a home security system? I approached the jar, twisted it open, and the pungent scent of herbs reached my nose. I looked away, returned again, over and over, until the scent became incredibly familiar. It smelled of pine, of greenery, of bitterness: it smelled of gin. A grin lined my face. Yes, there were the juniper berries–small, dark, dried fruits hidden amongst the other herbs. And there was mugwort–the soft fluffy parts contrasted with woody chunks. A piece of yarn hung around the mouth of the jar, a twig of rowan attached.

My grandmother associated these plants with intuition, prophecy. Was she suggesting that in times of alarm this tea should be consumed? Shouldn't someone who is alarmed take something calming?

That's not how my granny thought. Here, she was empowering the drinker to gain insight about their situation and to be proactive about it. She was never one to shy away from a problem.

I turned. There were many jars of this nature, jars labeled with emotions like BITTERNESS like DEFEAT like EMPTINESS. When I opened each jar, the corresponding herbs were there. My grandmother had created a complex pharmacy and had left it behind for us. I didn't recall these jars or these blends specifically. But, growing up, my grandmother had certainly given me many teas and I consumed them without thought. While other kids were guzzling Capri Sun or Juicy Juice, I would pause and gulp down my grandmother's warming concoction with a bit of shortbread before going outside to explore her vast yard and gardens.

I was amazed and overwhelmed by the huge collection. My eyes stopped when they landed on GRIEF.

The word glowed out at me from the dimness of the closet.

GRIEF. GRIEF.

Granny Sadie lived much longer than any doctor predicted. Over time she began to shrink, her back curling, her hands evolving into claws until she had difficulty using them. Yet, she still got up every day and tended to her plants and to her grandchildren. Despite all of the doctor's reports and warnings about the eventuality of death, we were all still shocked when it happened.

No more Granny.

When I got the call about her death, I continued to get dressed and went to work. It was surreal. As we worked through probate court, the words remained surreal. When I moved into her home, it was surreal.

All of her sweaters in a row. Her porcelain figures on the mantelpiece. The teapot that resided on the stove. The homegrown onions on the counter had begun sprouting, the greenery twisting through the air. Life carried on, but Granny did not.

GRIEF. GRIEF.

I opened the container and the sweetness of the apple blossoms hit me before I looked at them. The scent was overwhelmingly suffocating, and Granny's mysterious spicy perfume disappeared under it. I closed my eyes for a moment to take it in.

The image of the apple trees loomed out of the dark, like ghosts.

My eyes slowly opened, lazily found the contents of the jar. There were layers of dried blossoms and hunks of dried fruit, the juicy flesh shriveled to husks. Broken up sugar cubes were sprinkled throughout.

I envisioned my granny popping a sugar cube or two into my cuppa, even when mam told her to cut it out because I was getting too many cavities. *Life's too short,* she had whispered.

Tears blurred my eyes as I looked towards the jar again. Amongst the smell of the flowers, I cried for my granny. My tears started to hit the petals and I moved to close the jar before I ruined it.

But the drops caught something and I stopped myself before closing the lid.

What was that thing amongst the flowers?

I didn't want to touch the tea with my hands, let alone my tears.

I gently shook the canister until the item revealed itself. It was a piece of paper, and in pink ink it read my granddaddy's name.

I kept churning the canister and the names of dead relatives appeared–an uncle, the brother that died right after being born–names I had heard Granny speak that sounded foreign to my ears–then older words, words I did not know and felt too complicated for my mouth. I continued to churn aimlessly, looking into the flowers as they moved, a gentle wave carrying written messages in my grandmother's hand. The sugar cubes shifted, slowly hitting the glass bottom with soft noises. The heavy scent of the dried petals continued to waft to my face.

Why would Granny have put paper in one of her tea mixes? What were those ancient words, so quickly seen, now lost to the flowers? The questions came and went as I breathed deeply, and as the apple trees loomed out of the darkness of my mind.

Grief. Grief.

There were many things that remained untouchable in Granny's home, despite my name on the deed and my food in the fridge. The idea of reaching into that canister with the purpose of digging out the slips of paper seemed sacrilegious. Try as I might, after what seemed like many minutes of tossing the flowers, the words did not appear again. I fingered the twig from the apple tree that hung from the neck of the container. Apples. Apples. What had Granny taught me about them?

I knew Granny and Granddaddy planted the trees themselves and fostered them until they fruited several years later. She made an apple cake every Sunday, pooled in a warm custard sauce. My mouth watered at the thought; despite many attempts after her departure, it was one recipe I had been unable to get just right. She had taught me the recipe and I stood beside her many times, adding the cinnamon to the batter and combining the oats with the streusel topping. But perhaps there was something she added when I wasn't looking that she never disclosed to me. It seemed there were many things she hadn't left behind in her will.

A smile lined my face as another memory came in. After trick-or-treating in her neighborhood, I would come back to Granny's place bedecked in my princess gown. Granny never tried to force me out of it and would spend the night complimenting my beauty and calling me her royal highness. At first, the evening would start with me prancing about, nose in the air, the royal leader to my entourage of one. Once I was finished, Granny would make me some tea and we would sit, pinkies in the air, and drink it like ladies. An examination of the riches from my pillaging followed. My grandma favored chewy sweets, and my Twizzlers and Tootsie Rolls would magically disappear while I gobbled Butterfingers, my hands gaining their own chocolate coating.

After we discussed all the beautiful and scary costumes, we began our own celebration. My fingers would soon grow wet with orange pumpkin flesh while we dug out the guts and the seeds, which Granny saved to roast later on. The memory made me close my eyes and the buttery, salted crunch manifested in my mouth. The image of the pale apple tree loomed out of the dark at me yet again and I was startled by it, so I jumped, catching the tea container before I dropped it.

I continued to think about those late October nights while placing the jar back on the shelf. Granny would always tell me the story of Stingy Jack, and how we made the jack o'lantern to protect ourselves from any wandering evil spirits. Then she would take me by the hand and lead me to the apple trees.

My eyes opened and landed on the jar on the shelf, and one of the elusive scraps of paper looked back at me.

Saint Brandon stared back at me from the icon hung above Granny's altar. His eyes peered out of a face hallowed with age and half-covered with a wild, unruly beard. I stared at the wooden boat he held in his hands and the words of the rosary drifted up from my memory: ...*now and at the hour of death.*

I had not touched many things in Granny's home since I inherited it; I could still sense and smell her everywhere, the stench of mothballs hung heavy in her closet. I was periodically able to put away one or two items. My mother had suggested donating some of it, but I could not bear the idea—although I was not sure where everything would find a home, her attic and cellar already populated so many treasures.

But I had not touched any of her religious altars, or even considered it. Saint Brandon had stared down at me while I walked by every day, surrounded by half-burnt candles. I stared at the dark wicks, long and curled in the aftermath of heat. These could have been the last candles Granny ever lit; she would never light any again.

I reached out to touch them, to put my hands where hers had been. The wax felt cool and heavy and bumpy under my fingers, trails where it had dripped.

Sure, St. Brigid's eyes followed me every time I walked down the hall to Granny's room. Sure, the only times in my life Granny tried to straighten my hair were for church. I went but often lost myself in the droning of the service. Mom had worshiped at the bottle and had never really made a place for Jesus in our home.

Below Saint Brandon's gaze were the candles, and a small wooden boat. I struggled to remember what this Saint watched over, but nothing came to me. If I were honest, I wasn't even sure what the more famous Brigid protected–I just knew her as the cloaked woman.

Besides the boat, a pile of twigs gathered from Granny's apple tree. A prayer card.

Help me to journey, beyond the familiar into the unknown...

Every Halloween, Granny took me out under the apple trees. We dug into the earth, which was firming up but hadn't reached frozen just yet. We would place an apple into the hole.

Granny was not a strict teacher; when she taught me about her brews or her bakes, she allowed me to do only as much as I wanted. If I ran off, uninterested, she would give me a candy or a baked good. But Halloween was one of the only times she would make me focus.

She cradled her hand under my chin, her eyes looking into my own. I would only realize later that I had inherited those blue eyes, amongst many other things.

We always feed the dead on this night...

We would cover the apple with soil. She would send me inside, asking me to light a candle in the kitchen window. I would look at the way the apple trees loomed out of the dark before sparking the flame

I was never brave enough to join Granny after that. I wasn't sure if she wanted me to. The talk of spirits made me afraid. I would return to my candy, often allowing myself one of the sweets Granny preferred. A feeling of wrongness would continue to descend on me.

I would run up the stairs without looking behind me and dive into bed, my costume still on and tangled around my thin ankles.

It was one of the only times I voluntarily clutched the rosary, repeating the words before I fell asleep.

Saint Brandon. Patron of travelers. Bran mac Febail, that ancient traveler. Men who went out seeking other realms. Men who were beckoned by otherworldly women.

Halloween crept closer and closer. A day when the veil is thin, when it can be traveled across.

Where had Granny been traveling to, out amongst the trees? How much wisdom did that pantry contain?

As the days approached Halloween, I realized it was something Granny had never really trained me for. She had taught me how to make beef stew and bannock. I knew how to brew any style of tea so it was steeped just right, without becoming bitter. I knew how to combine herbs and oil, how to slather them over the aching parts of bodies to make pain melt away.

But I did not know how to travel: the farthest I had ever been was Granny's backyard here in rural upstate. It felt completely foreign to Mom's house in the city built on the backs of bottles. Granny always welcomed us, or most often, me—we would bake and she told me stories. Someone finally saw me, finally listened. I was loved and I was safe and I was free to roam the grounds.

Sure, I had climbed those apple trees over a million times; I had plucked their fruit and buried my face in their flowers.

But had I ever really truly looked and seen them?

The internet told me that the ancient Celts believed there was a magical apple branch that could transport you to the other side.

But where, where would it take you? Granny's heaven, or something much more ancient?

Granny always taught me that we are a strange people, Catholics that still relied on the plants for their medicine.

But which was true? Was it both?

I found myself stopping at Saint Brandon's altar and reciting the prayer on his card whenever I passed.

Give me the faith to leave old ways and break fresh ground with you...

Where would this journey take me?

I entered the pantry over and over, churning the jar of flowers, a blend of names appearing to me.

Who would I see on that night, out there in the dark? Who would I see?

I continued to pray. My prayer often involved sitting in Granny's pantry, closing my eyes, and taking in the spicy scent.

I repeated Brandon's prayer over and over.

When the night came, his words lined my mouth. I found my way to the trees in the dark. The moon was small, but I knew my way after all those years. The trees loomed bright from the dark. The trees loomed.

As I approached I plucked a fresh apple from a branch. The dead deserved the best. I dug into earth that was harder than I expected, but I should have known better. It was cold; I had worn one of Granny's old sweaters. I could smell her on it–not that unknown spicy smell, but the smell of her shampoo and the sweetness of talcum powder and I started crying over and over again; she was so close yet so far. I grasped a rock and started going deeper into the soil. I had been chanting Brandon's name at first but it faded to Granny's name, Granny Granny Granny....

I buried the apple, her old words leaving my mouth: *I bury this apple to feed my dead....*

I sat on the hard ground. I lit the candle from Saint Brandon's altar. I gripped the apple tree branch. I closed my eyes. I allowed the identity of being Catholic only by family lineage drop; I let everything drop, all defenses. Tears continued to pour down my face. Yes, the house was a blessing, but also a curse: to live so close to her, yet so far. I buried my face in the sweater and breathed in the smell of her again. She had been the only person to truly see me, or to even take the time to try. Now I lived in this huge house alone. Time was slipping by. I was getting older. Would anyone ever notice me again? Would I eventually find a husband in a bottle, as my mother had done?

Granny, Granny, Granny...

My hands clutched the branch. What would my future hold? On this night, in the long run? What was left for me? What ever had been? A sad little girl pickled in her mother's liquor, left alone and bullied and longing for Granny? There was no more Granny, there was no more Granny, there was no more.

I heard the distinctive step, followed by the long pause as she swung her bad hip, the thud as the cane hit the ground.

The ancient Celts called Halloween Samhain and they believed it was when the veil was at its thinnest and that we could reach over to the other side, if only we took the time and tried.

Help me to journey, beyond the familiar into the unknown...

The rasp of her voice was as dry as the leaves as she joined me in prayer.

Linden's Legends

ZQ Taylor

ZQ Taylor is a Silicon Valley tech writer by day and budding novelist and essayist by night. She has written for local and national publications, including InFlight USA Magazine, The Daily Astorian, and Park Ave Magazine. ZQ has been described as a southern belle in combat boots, charming and disarming.

ZQ Taylor: The Indelible Storyteller

Rumor, when properly tended, becomes legend.

Rumor has it that I descend from gods and royals, lovers and virgins, and the hands of two bloods, red and white. Through eternity, my kin fostered opulent legends and epic reverence.

Maybe you know of the princess who fled her father's kingdom to become a devout hermit performing miracles from the base of a tree? Or of Zeus transforming a dying couple, who were still vibrantly in love, into two trees, their branches forever intertwined? Or perhaps you've read Eminescu's timeless poems, all written from underneath a fabled tree?

Not to brag, but I hail from a botanastic dynasty that goes by many names. Through millennia, robust branches have thrived in Europe and Asia, across British Isles, Nordic mountains, and Romanian parks. Our crowns are lofty and lush, our roots deep and resolute. Our rings are adorned not in gold or diamonds, but with flowers and honey.

We are the guardians of secrets and the purveyors of truth. I can decipher encrypted birdsong, conceal nests and children, and capture the wind's whispers. My awning has sheltered the righteous, bristled against bias, and nurtured soulmates.

The American Tilia Branch is my direct line, with kissing cousins Little-Leaf, Tomentosa, and Henryana, who goes by Henry's Lime. I have been called Basswood, Beetree, and Silver, but please, just call me Linden.

Every tree has a story. Mine has enchanted entire forests.

Rhapsody in Spring

As a young sprout, my world was an impeccable, dense kaleidoscope of green. Rain serenaded the grass, and I swayed to catch dewdrops. Frogs added percussion. Bright lime parakeets and treehoppers darted between Spring shoots. Even the powdery smooth caresses of emerald moths on olive milkweed vines pulsed with pigment. I still recall the unforced rhythms of that Green Grace as if it were yesterday...

Oh! What is that wriggling ball of dandelion fuzz? It's floppy and coming my way! No, there are three floppy dandelions!

My neighbor is a brooding Oak tree. He tells me these are bunnies—cuddly wild animals, not plants like us.

Oh! Wait for me! I want to play with the dandelion bunnies. So, I brandish my leaves and stretch my roots to join in their frolic. My seed may be sown, but my spirit is liberated.

Wait! Where are you going? They are flopping to the canopies of Cottonwood codgers huddled by the river. I'll have a great canopy one day, and then the bunnies will hop and rest with me.

...With those earliest memories came the joy of seedling wonder. My roots were not yet well-developed, but I was grounded in my forest family and the knowing that I was conceived with hope. Let me tell you more...

Woodland fairies sing stories of two bloods planting my seed, of a nobleman and a warrior meeting at the river yonder. The gentleman tells of mythical Lindens that hold a divine presence, promote healing, and under which no lie can be told. The warrior speaks to his noble friend of a place to honor the Peacemaker and the Eagle so that this shared land will be rooted in harmony and winged with wisdom.

These two humans sow unity as fresh as the new colonies. They hunt and share meals. The warrior's woman tucks me in at night with rich tapestries of soil and prayers. I grow strong and straight.

One day, the gentleman brings his wife, who has a seed growing in her stomach. The gentleman and Milady spread a blanket beside my burgeoning arbor to laugh and dream. Tapestries and dreams become the light that sustains me. Way better than dandy floppies.

When I reach ten rings of age, I overhear the brazen gossip of the breeze. The winds blow warnings of angry locusts carrying rifles and a Trail of Tears flowing just past my purview, on a bloody horizon. Whatever that means.

Weeks go by, and no one comes to tuck me in or daydream. Rains pour, unrelenting in their extravagant sorrow. The warriors are gone, forced to sprout in a gaunt, far-away land. The gentleman becomes a reluctant soldier and soldiers on.

Surely, my conceivers will come home. I wait. Any season now. I hope. I believe.

Expectations have a funny way of unraveling, leaving nothing except bare truths. The reality is they never return, I am orphaned, and my world tints in colorless shards of darkness.

Evergreens hum courage, but my forest frivolity falls away, and I slip into deciduous doldrums. The annoying mighty Oak reveals that possibilities are endless when we rotate our perspective simply by moving into the light. Huh? Ignoring my teenage naiveté, he quips something about 'within dormancy lies great potential.' For what, I wonder.

Time snatches precious hours. Before I know it, I have become a snarky sapling looking for a way to high-five the sky. My impatience to grow up does nothing to trellis my height. I don't find it particularly exciting to twiddle my twigs until the growing season arrives. Crickets incessantly clacking their crochet needles are not music to my ears. Even the arrival of white-tailed deer in the clearing fails to quell my rebellious boredom to grow already.

Well, dormancy delivers, but not in the way I expect. One bleak night, the noble soldier's wife staggers through our woods in a virulent sleet storm. Milady rests her head on my burrowing roots and sobs for the great loves she has lost—first her husband and now her sapling son.

My branches droop with grief, and I shelter Milady as best I can through the freezing storm. I can do nothing but absorb her dying tears. I call to the Legends for divine healing. I shout for creatures of the forest to come when they can. The fierce gale strangles my cries for help.

In the blue light of morning, an enormous eagle lands on my crest, and I buckle under its hefty talons, but only for a moment. His magical prowess instantly warms my soggy soul to a golden glow. Sparrows sound reveille. Floppies and wild parakeets come to fill the crevices between Milady's lifeless branches and mine. The woodland fairies thank me for my bravery and sprinkle Milady with forget-me-nots and jasmine petals. Migrant swarms of bees pollinate and fructify. Milady's spirit awakens as if from slumber, hugs me, and vanishes into every sprig of my being.

This same day, I celebrate my fifteenth ring with a five-o-clock shadow and six whole inches in height. Sun shines down and dries the last of my rankled leaves. I feel the earthly cadence of being whole. I am no longer an orphan, a sapling. I have become the kaleidoscope, not just with shades of green, but with all the colors of the forest. High-five, big sky!

Cicadas of Summer

Once upon a time, right in the middle of an ordinary life, Love gives us a fairy tale.

We are decades into our new country, and my embryonic inno-cence has ripened to a compact sanctuary of shade. Farmlands and hamlets have amputated acres of our lush forest. Humans traipse back and across the wildflower meadows in between. And a young man arrives one afternoon. He stares up at me, smiles, and grips my trunk.

How odd the sensation as he climbs me! My ample branches tickle as he brushes leaves and buds. I blush and blossom in hues of yellow. He rests a bit and swings his long legs and threadbare shoes to a beat of his own. Then, the teen climbs down and sprints away, calling out, "I'll be back!"

You know that romance festers in the rage of summer, right?

I was giddy. The poetry of how he woke me—the lustrous feel-ing of connection. Dusk understands, working escort duty for the screeching cacophony of mating cicadas—oh my Mother Nature, they are loud! As the moon ripples over the river and the sky changes into its sleeping clothes, I pine for the reappearance of my mysterious friend.

The next twilight, he returns. With a pretty young lady. Golden twisty vines frame her pale face, and surely, she embodies

Freyja, the goddess of love and beauty. Delicate fingers trace over a bulbous warty limb of mine. I swear, I bloom ten-fold this very moment.

Garrett and Wista. Together, they climb and swing and kiss. Garrett and Wista, sitting in the tree, K-I-S-S-I-N-G. Someone calls from far away, and Miss Wista hurries to go despite the cicadas' deafening chicanery. She kisses Garrett and hugs me.

We three are in love.

Every day, Garrett waits with me for Wista. This is no seedling love—it has the purity and honor of Evergreen. Each time they kiss and cajole, I flourish with sweet honey and perfect flowers. Garrett wears his heart on his sleeve, and I don all of mine: Lindens have heart-shaped leaves!

Cicadas regale us nightly. Virtuosos of love songs. Garrett harmonizes with big plans to conquer industry while Wista sketches fanciful wonders in moss-green charcoal. Sometimes she whispers wild wishes in his ear. But the distant call of home always comes, and dutifully she always goes.

Garrett pleads with her to start a life together without the confines of her family's money or his lack of it. He will be here tomorrow, ready to go into the Big World. It will be summer solstice, a lucky day for love. Garrett's parting kiss beckons her to join him.

The next day, Wista does not show. We wait for her. Garrett carefully wedges the promise ring into his waistcoat pocket and climbs higher than ever. He peers through my dappled cushion, hoping to glimpse a sign of the golden goddess walking toward us. All we can see are her family's neat rows of grapevines laden with rich purples.

We wait in the loud quiet of the darkening woods. Nocturnal

choirs of cicadas bewitch even fireflies to light the way for Wista. But she never comes. Eventually, a gentle fog blankets us with sleep.

Morning startles me. Garrett is gone, but he's left a letter in my bark folds. The promise ring hangs by a shoelace from my warty branch.

All day, bees frenzy in their celestial dance, yet I mope, and my flowers slouch. It really does feel like the longest cavalcade of the year. By sundown, I wave away the honeybees and embrace nesting birds and vibrating cicadas.

Must we all just play our part in the world? Does Fate skewer the stars of lovers with no hope for a happy ending? Garrett has wings of an eagle, willing to find his way in the world, but Wista roots her worth in the levy of family. I gloom.

Constellations toast the solstice carnival like champagne and cabaret upon the night sky. And that's when I see her, our dazzling impressionist's flower, ascending the hill to me. Wista quickly finds Garrett's note and band of gold. At once, she crumples, weeps, and leaves—

—Now, now, cheer up! I am the Tree of Lovers, and I promised a fairytale.

That night, the cicadas abruptly vanish, their viral whir gone. What humans may not know is that cicadas, like pure love and good wine, can burrow and mature in the vigor of soil for years. The fermentation of faith.

Eventually, Wista returns with a wine bottle and Garrett's parting gifts. The vineyard's new indigo label shows a profile of hair swirling around a sad, cherubic face shedding tears. Her father had aptly named the prized wine Wista Weeps.

Through inebriated grief, my Wista does indeed weep. She marshals Garrett's note and ring into the emptied bottle—her liquid heartache splashing—and buries it beneath my hulking roots with a prayer. I guard her hidden treasure like teeth under a pillow, wishing for root fairies to grant her wish.

Years go by. Concentric circles swell my girth, and Wista continues to visit after work. She wearies from the stronghold of her duties. She nurtures her grapes like babies, each vine swaddled and fed and guided. Even her hair and fingers absorb the inky tints of her labor.

Then, one night her father dies, and the winery is hers. She skips up the hill in the middle of the day, mourning dress flowing, coiffed hair unraveling. She speaks of messaging the Big World into which Garrett had ventured, with hopes of retrieving her only love.

Her missive—Wista Waits—dispatches with smashing success, selling in places her imagination could only conjure. Unlike previous labels of melancholy blue, the latest bottle boasts a happy moss-green sketch of our dear girl sitting under my fullest plume and holding a ring on a string.

The smells of summer harvest our hopes. I lace twigs to cradle fuzzy fledglings and bustle with bees to make honey. Voluptuous grapes spill from vines. And Wista arrives nightly with her unshackled smile. Together we wait.

And then, just like that, seventeen years from the night she buried her love and laughter, millions of cicadas burst forth from fermented ground. Their ballad pounds the threshold of human hearing.

Only they knew what a momentous occasion lay ahead.

Wista feels the vineyard flutter. She marvels as bruise-purple grapes suddenly blanch to spirals of ethereal gold as if polished by Moon. Her hair and fingertips gloss translucent.

She knows. He is here.

Garrett has returned from his worldly travels. Clammy hands belie the sensibilities of his long legs and fine leather shoes. He sets down the bouquet of exotic flowers and a case of precious Wista Waits. Message received loud and clear: Love potion, bottled just for him. He pats his waistcoat.

The entire valley holds its collective breath. Wista races up the hill, Garrett down. They mesh and mash in the middle and laugh and cry. He drops to his knees with a shiny new ring, and every blade of grass undulates in her yes.

Their wedding is held under my branches. Birds and neighbors string ribbons, a preacher blesses the union, and wine flows like the burly river.

Garrett buys the lands framing my roots in every direction. He builds a castle for his bride and a treehouse for their children. My flowers fill their vases, my honey their pots. Evenings are spent dancing to the "cicadian" rhythms under the stars. We are in love.

Gilded for Autumn

Nature never fails to wow us. She spins magical legacies with each returning season, casts dewy realms of beauty for every creature. Treetop crowns are bejeweled with leaves of brick red, bright orange, and honeyed blonde. In this otherworldly chroma of autumn, our leaves may change, but our purpose is the same: to live in harmony with the world around us and to embrace the audacity of transformation.

Firmly planted in the twentieth century, my world now spans a massive public park, mostly manicured yet softly wild from my backside down to the beloved river. The crotchety Oak is still bent in his ways, and a trio of fast-growing, smooth-talking Red Maples brightens the landscape. I admit my spine has some curvature, too, and a few branches pose in downward dog. But I am young at heart.

Life is good.

Most autumn days, our lawns are peopled with promenades and prams, picnics and parades. By evening, I sway to the nearby clickety-clack of railways—and the billowy warble of Jazz. Here, the nights belong to Tristan, a ten-year-old musical wonder.

Tristan has many siblings and a singular talent. He plays saxophone below my gilded leaves. He floats above the music. His melodies hypnotize birdsong and can charm bark from trees. Even the high-speed squirrels skittering me like a May Day pole suspend their harassment whenever Tristan tongues his saxophone.

You'd believe the boy and the sax are one, that they can levitate Time—well, if not for the kudzu. With every ghost and swell of Tristan's saxophone, the trespassing vines twist around unsuspecting shrubs and boughs, mine included. Our leaves dance until they drop, spent from the glory of Tristan's tunes.

Word of the boy maestro spreads like pollen. Variegated crowds come to appreciate music under stars. To gyrate rhythm beneath branches. To tap toes and clap hands. Curious performers arrive from nearby juke joints, country clubs, and church choirs to improvise and pizz with the kid. And tendrils of kudzu party like social climbers along my shedding canopy.

Each evening, a regal but raisined man trudges past us, gold pocket watch screaming his lateness, soundless sadness wrinkling him more. Then, one night, those Red Maple sirens elbow the man to pay attention. He looks up. Perks up. His finely tailored scowl stretches to a gaping smile at Tristan's tweedy tempo.

The man flushes to tears. You see, his wife had played the saxophone long ago, apparently with Adolphe Sax himself at the Paris Opera. While Tristan's rolling swing differs from her laced-up solos, Mister hears the same ardent soul. Tristan's sax throbs with shocking long-notes like kisses of perpetuity. And Mister feels the pecks of joy he used to share with the missus.

After the performance, Mister approaches Tristan's proud but weary parents, inquiring about the boy's musical education. Mama declares that Tristan just started playing the second-hand saxophone her husband dabbled at before they were parents. Papa concedes that his focus is on feeding mouths, not dreams.

Mister reveals he has money and connections, and until now, has had no joie de vivre since his wife died. He offers to sponsor Tristan, to get his talent on the sheet and in concert halls. Mama cautions they have no money for lessons, but the man insists the lad's talent is generational.

So, after Tristan's school and chores, several evenings a week, the patron pens the prodigy's genius to paper. Tristan signs his work, and Mister flails brilliant pages to urban orchestras.

The great conservatoires hesitate to offer Tristan scholarships or apprenticeships. Sure, they believe he has talent, but he is just a boy. The saxophone is just a fad. Mister whisks here and there undeterred in his pursuit.

Meanwhile, Tristan mesmerizes the growing frenzy of fans

under my gangly tentacles. Flirting kudzu and flatulent trains keep beat. The wanton Red Maples shimmy. And I shake and molt my crinkly detritus like a writer frantically penning and crumpling sheaves of paper to get his letter just right. It is impossible to stand still.

Until it isn't.

The glisten of our jubilant togetherness evaporates one scary, moonless night. The train is robbed, the air smells of evil, and the crowds shutter at home. The thieves use the desolate darkness to their advantage, shoveling behind my trunk to hide loaded bags of passenger loot until a morning get-away. I struggle to bend and swat them away. To no avail.

In the nearing distance, I see Tristan and Mister prickle against the scratch of jagged wind as they head my way. No! Stop! Don't they know to stay home? This is when I notice Tristan's saxophone leaning against the front of my trunk. He must have left it when hurrying home from school for chores before lessons with Mister.

Why, Moon, did you choose this night to go AWOL? And where is the crisp gentleness of equinox? What cruel trick is this to make me shelter the wicked?

Tristan and Mister are at my roots.

Tristan grabs his sax before he sees the thugs. Mister's wrinkly reflexes brazen anew as he valiantly protects the boy. One of the criminals makes haste with his shovel, smashing Mister to the ground and heading for my lad. But Tristan wails his sax with fierce vibrato, and the thieves freeze—just long enough for the kudzu to leap from my limbs and lasso theirs.

Mister stirs, yet Tristan is too stunned to stop playing. Each fiery note commands the muscular kudzu to manacle the monsters. The wind takes notice, directing shrapnel-sharp squall upon the treachery. Heavens conscript Moon to illuminate the path for townspeople rushing up the hill.

In moments that feel like tree rings, the thieves are apprehended, evil has ended, and Mister is mended. Splendid.

Tristan's family crowd and hug him, coaxing the saxophone from his shaking fingers. But the saxophone does not let go.

The pink pucker of morning bathes our park. Kudzu vines slink down from branches, sweetly raking my crusty gold leaves into piles. Kids run and dive into the heaps. Music directors and orchestra conductors preen and puffer with offers. Tristan and his saxophone play for them all.

The journey for our young friend and his gold-plated appendage globetrots for decades. Tristan and his saxophone pack theaters, concert halls, and nightclubs around the world. The whiz kid makes records with major labels and famous crooners. Everywhere he travels, saxomania follows.

Tristan always makes it home in the fall. He delights local crowds. My periphery has gained wrought-iron benches and picnic tables and has lost its heroic kudzu. Tristan's family and elderly patron horde front rows.

Autumns later, Mister is buried next to his wife. His final wish is to have his service under my awning, the very place his soul had reawakened. At the memorial, Tristan extolls tender blues for his dear benefactor.

On this day, the festooned crowns of my fellow trees fade to terra cotta and burnished brass. Except those racy Red Maples—they are as feisty and vibrant as ever.

Perhaps because I am Tristan's forever friend, because his music was born under my branches, on this day, my gilded livery transforms to 24-karat gold dust. And floats above the music.

Wisdom of Winter

Nearly three centuries have varnished me with love, friendship, and understanding. And from nose to tail, I now stand at least 100 squirrels in height. In the winter of my long life, I breathe deep and rest in the majesty of knowing. My boughs are barren in the season's stark splendor and fertile with wisdom even the eagle would envy.

Through the years, I have been everywhere without ever leaving home. From my branches, year-round cardinals chide prodigal snowbirds returning with tales of hardship and adventure. Generations of deer and floppies usher curious offspring into my grasp to learn how to grow strong and clever. At the base of my gnarled roots, talented artists, students and scientists chronicle my time and selfie their own.

In winter, no tree is dying. Not really. Instead, we enjoy a much needed respite during the shorter days and subdued activities. As I wait for Sun's waning temperature to warm the corrugated folds of my soul, I reflect.

Memories ripple as if across icy river waters, frozen in time and flowing just the same. I recall so many trees, some cut down in their prime, others aged and pulpy. Many live on as the cherished pages of books—and the shelves that house them. Others make music as instruments or provide shelter.

Lindens live on in the legacies of story.

Over time, I've discovered a lot. I know that even in an ebbing woodland, beauty sprouts from ashes. I see everything change and nothing change. And I recognize that while growth happens, maturity is optional.

I have also learned to value the big importance of small things. The frosted tranquility of my meadows. The clamoring silence of snow—each snowflake thrums through the air with keen resolve to join the greater assembly, not melt alone.

Like snowflakes and fingerprints, every leaf in all the world throughout infinity is unique. No two are alike. But I think we are all the same in that we differ. That we each have our own purpose. That we matter.

Together, we are legends in our own right.

The Mother Tree

Elana Gomel

Corinne knocked on her mother's door. It was quiet inside; only the soft susurrus of growing mats and the slither of the walls answered her. When she pressed her ear to the smooth warm wood, she could hear a rapid whisper, but she was not sure whether it was coming from inside the house or inside her. Her heavy belly was dragging her down, so she leaned against the wall. The riot of flowering vines above her head poured down the fragrance of hot amber, making her nauseous. One of the half-opened flowers, orange pink with a convoluted scarlet heart, dipped down, its folded petals caressing her cheek.

"Mama!" her daughter said, her soft voice penetrating Corinne's muscles and bones, carried on the tide of her blood. She pretended not to hear.

"Mama!" More insistent now. Corinne stared into the indigo sky, the sun barely peeping above the tops of fruit trees in the plantation, gilding their upthrust limbs with the rosy morning light. Beyond the plantation, the dense thicket of pitcher trees was barely visible: just an occasional flicker of a thick orange tongue, as the waking plants licked their fleshy speckled lips. On the other side, the village sloped down to the endless marshland, slivers of water sparkling like pieces of a broken mirror.

Her left leg twitched. Corinne squeezed her thigh, leaving red fingermarks in the bronze flesh. The twitch subsided, but then her right leg moved. Like the hand of a puppeteer inside the puppet, her daughter was moving her body.

"What do you want?" she yelled so loudly that her throat hurt. There was no need to; her daughter could read her thoughts - at least those articulated in words. But it gave Corinne a bitter satisfaction to punish the body that was no longer her own.

"Mama." Her daughter's inner voice set Connie's nerves on edge. "Look up."

Connie did. Stamped on the silky wood of the upper doorframe was the sigil of the Children's Council: a stylized human figure with its feet debouching into a network of roots.

"No!" Connie cried and beat on the door, as if she could make time run backward by sheer exertion. The furled flower buds on the roof shuddered, getting ready for their task.

"Nana is no longer here," her daughter said. "We should visit her in the plantation."

"It's too early!" Corinne insisted. "She is not supposed to be there!"

Her daughter, who would now have a name, was silent. Corinne swallowed the bitter tears of futility. There was no schedule for rooting, at least not for women. Men went early, of course, having fulfilled their biological function. But some women remained mobile even after having grandchildren. Aliana, Corinne's mother, had seemed to be of this kind: her grandson was almost into puberty, and she still smiled at Corinne and made her a snack when she came for a visit. Corinne had somehow convinced herself that the laws of nature would make an exception for the tight bond between mother and daughter. More fool, she!

Corinne turned away from the house and hurried toward the plantation, her pregnant belly jiggling under her loose shift. Behind her, the house sagged and unraveled. The vines on the roof opened up into explosions of electric pink and deep scarlet, their crimson-dappled stems squeezing the thin wooden walls until they collapsed into a pile of splinters. The thatched roof caved in. The still-growing mats on the floor inched away like flattened caterpillars. A new house would grow here when the Children's Council decided it was time for a growing toddler to have their own home, apart from their mother whose services they no longer needed. But Corinne did not look back at the destruction of her childhood home. She ran as fast as she could, buoyed by the desperate hope of seeing her mother one last time.

"Don't run, Mama!" her daughter cried through the drumming of her heart. "You're making me sick!"

"Deal with it!" Corinne snarled. "You can't tell me what to do! You still have no name."

"My name is Aliana."

"No. Not yet."

The verge of the plantation was marked by a shallow ditch. Beyond it, the grassy plain where the village stood was abruptly supplanted by the green dusk of the many gnarled and contorted trunks, their branches twined and straining against each other. It was not healthy to plant so many elders in such a small space but there was no choice: the village was squeezed in between the protective pitcher tree forest and the marshland. The floating people, who cultivated their own elders in the form of bony cattails with a harvest of tough drupes, had no love of the villagers—and the feeling was mutual. Peony, Corinne's settled village, was contemptuous of the rafts and boats of the floating people who shamelessly supplemented their diet with fish and snails. But there was no denying that they prospered and encroached on Peony's land, making it imperative that the plantation had enough fruit-bearing trees.

A swift kick in Corinne's ribs make her double up in pain. Her daughter was angry.

Corinne straightened up, taking long slow breaths, and forcing herself to withdraw from her own body, taking refuge in a small, protected spot in her brain where she was still herself. As her body was being taken over by her unwanted offspring, her mind was dropping parts of itself like a wilting flower dropping petals. In her sapling years, she had been the best in her grade at reading. Now it would take her several hours to read a single page. Her son Edward could read fluently, having inherited her knack, but she did not begrudge him this skill, stolen from her when he was in her womb. He was a boy, doomed to a short blooming and early senescence, following immediately by his fructifying a girl or two. Corinne's own chosen partner, Arthur, father of Edward, had rooted long ago. Partners were not family, but Connie, contrarian as always, had visited him several times, gazing in silence at the glaucous mask of his face being slowly absorbed into the bark of the tree he had become.

The sun climbed higher into the sky, diluting its deep blue into the faded white of another hot day. Corinne's shift was glued to her body by perspiration. The girl inside her lapsed into a sullen silence and stopped kicking. Beneath her feet, the living grass quaked and crawled, its tough stems weaving together into long green snakes that spasmed, trying to pull their roots out of the crumbly soil. The backs of the snakes erupted into the froth of small white and yellow flowers. Ahead of her, an orchid as tall as herself swayed gently in the still air, back and forth, with a hypnotic grace. This was a Queen Orchid, the babymaker. Its thick yellow petals, spotted with red and black. turned toward Connie, the tubular protrusion in the middle shuddering, ripe with pollen. But sensing the life in Connie's uterus, the orchid lost interest and the blossom folded. Connie spat into the grass. An orchid like this one was responsible for her pregnancy. She had fought hard, remaining single and abstaining from sex since Edward's birth. But one whiff of a Queen Orchid's pollen, and she had rushed out to grab the first available boy whose name she did not remember. Spitefully, she hoped he would be rooting by now.

Her mouth furry with thirst, Corinne finally made it into the shade of the plantation. The trees on the margin were the oldest ones, their human features all but gone. Still, she paused, her hand resting on the smooth green bark of the nearest elder. She could not even tell whether it had been a man or a woman, though their family would know. The trunk was knobby and squat, woody muscles bunching up under the cool tegument. The long flexible branches erupting into a shaggy crown just above Corinne's head stirred lazily, the inverted cups of beige flowers at their ends dripping nectar. The face had all but melted into the trunk, only shallow indentations marking the eyes and the mouth, still opened in the "O" of a scream. Why were elders always screaming when planted? Wasn't it supposed to be the reward of a life well-lived—the green peace of being one with the land?

Corinne's mouth twitched into a derisive smile as she made her way deeper into the plantation, slowly cooling off. The lacy shadows of the branches dappled the ground with broken pieces of sunshine. She was surrounded by the slow exhalation of the elders whose photosynthesis purified the air breathed by their descendants and whose sweet nectar and ripening fruit fed their children and grandchildren. When Corinne was in school, she wrote a poem praising the beauty of the life cycle. She remembered it with shame. She would like to pen a very different poem now, but her kids had robbed her of the ability to write.

The trees were becoming more recognizable as individuals the closer she got to the center. Elders could move, slowly and painfully, dragging their roots out of the soil at night and migrating to the edge of the plantation as they grew older. Those on the outer edge would eventually be recycled into implements or in severe winters, burned. Matches were strictly controlled by the Council, and no adult was allowed to possess them.

And here was her mother.

Aliana stood in the middle of a small clearing; her head bowed. Her feet were planted in the rich black soil, and a large earthworm crawled leisurely over her leg, its slimy pink head poking at the flesh, inspecting it for the future like a cook inspecting a basketful of vegetables. Her twig fingers still clutched her dress to her changing body in the last-ditch attempt at modesty. The thin fabric was stretched and torn by the erupting branches.

She lifted her head when her daughter ran into the clearing, the woody flesh of her neck creaking. Her face had begun its transition into a glassy mask that would eventually be absorbed into the trunk of the tree she was becoming. The skin was glassy-smooth and faintly greenish. The crow's feet and laugh-lines had disappeared. The dark blue eyes, Aliana's pride, rare in the village where most people, including Corinne, had nut-brown or black eyes, were glued shut. The black curls that Corinne had inherited were falling out, carpeting the soil.

Corinne leaned against the trunk and put her arms around it.

She remembered her own time in her mother's womb vividly. Like all fetuses, she acquired full sentience in the fifth month of pregnancy, waking up in the warm salty darkness with her head brimming with words and concepts. And there was her mother's regular heartbeat: the music of safety and protection. And then there were her mother's words, blooming in her brain like a shower of stars. *Welcome, little Corinne.*

Aliana had been much younger than Corinne was now. And she had been bright and cheerful, convinced, against all reason, that her unborn daughter would not chip away at her humanity. They had bonded while Corinne was in utero; and this bond persisted after she was born. This unnatural connection was one reason why Corinne, despite her obvious intelligence at birth, had never been drafted to serve on the Children's Council, composed of the smartest babies, toddlers, and kids. Until their intelligence started to wane around the age of seven, they ran the village's affairs. Even later in her life, as a sapling, Corinne remained an unpopular and lonely girl. But she had not minded her exclusion. Her mother, miraculously preserving her humanity even into her thirties, had always been her best friend.

And now, her mother was disappearing into green silence, and no matter how fiercely Corinne tried to hold her, Aliana was slipping away.

Her recalcitrant lips twitched as she tried to shape words but no matter how close Corinne leaned in, she could not make them out.

Until she could.

"Kill me!"

***

Edward was sprawling on the lawn in front of their house, reading a book. Books were considered morbid. They were corpses of trees; the processed flesh of the elders. They were needed to preserve basic knowledge but every year, the Children's Council voted down the number of permits for utilizing the dead.

Her daughter was silent in her womb, sensing Corinne's simmering anger. She would be on the Council, of course! A cocky brat, self-righteous and convinced of her immortality; she was made for the Council whose members were recruited the moment they were weaned. Corinne's only consolation was that her daughter would get her comeuppance when the time came for her to bear fruit. But Corinne knew how unlikely it was she would survive until then with enough mind left intact to feel schadenfreude.

Edward's face lit up with a smile when he saw his mother. He still lived with her, but their days of togetherness were numbered. His voice had begun to break. In less than a year, he would be assigned a partner to fructify and then his slide into vegetable mindlessness would be swift and assured.

Corinne sat by his side and put an arm around his shoulder. Behind them, the flowers on the roof of their house whispered in hissy voices like a bunch of mean girls.

"What are you reading?" Corinne asked her son to forestall his inquiry about his Nana. A shifty expression passed over Edward's face. He made a futile attempt to hide the book behind his back, but Corinne snatched it away.

The book was innocuous enough: a collection of recipes for grilling vegetables. Corinne was surprised that Edward would be interested in something so mundane, but he loved reading and would grab any book he could lay his hands on.

She leafed through the worn pages, shuddering when she thought of her mother's flesh eventually pulped into another cookbook.

One page was marked with a dogear. Corinne could not read the entirety of it but what she grasped was enough.

"It's a crime, Edward," she whispered.

Edward's lips trembled.

"And burying people in dirt and eating their tumors is not a crime?" he cried. "Telling me I'm only good for fucking and dying is not a crime? Making my Nana into a tree is not a crime?"

Corinne clamped her hand against his mouth. But it was too late: the flowers on the house had heard them, and so did the baby in her womb. Her daughter was silent, but Corinne had no illusions about where her loyalties lay.

"It's the cycle of life, Edward," she said, hating her own hypocrisy.

Edward wriggled away from her and looked at her with disdain.

"You know it's not true!" he shouted. "Everybody knows it's not true, but you're all too scared or too brainless to say it. Because the Earth was dying and there was no food, the Ancients did something to our genes: crossed humans with plants to make us live in 'harmony with nature!' Harmony! What a joke! So, don't give me this bullshit about the cycle of life! They screwed up and I'm paying the price!"

And before Corinne could say anything, he ran away, disappearing into the fragrant labyrinth of the village's flower- and vine-overflowing streets. Corinne took a deep breath.

"I'll strangle you if you tell on your brother," she sub-vocalized to the baby in her womb.

"Why do you love him more than me?" her daughter asked.

Corinne frowned. She had never thought to compare her children in this way.

"Because my mother is dying," she finally said. "You took her life, as you are taking mine. And now you want to take her name."

"But I didn't ask to be born," her daughter cried voicelessly, and Corinne had nothing to say because it was true.

She picked up the book again, her lips moving as she read it, syllable by recalcitrant syllable.

"How to make fire without matches."

***

Her water broke when she made a V-shaped notch in a wooden board and started collecting dry moss for tinder.

Corinne stared at the viscous puddle at her feet, grinding her teeth, and trying to push back against the unrelenting pressure in her lower abdomen. A spasm went through her body as if somebody grabbed a handful of her guts and twisted them.

"No!" she yelled at her daughter. "You are premature! You'll be born sickly and die soon!"

Her daughter did not reply. Grimly, she pushed her way out of the prison of Corinne's womb, turning around and getting ready to launch herself through the birth canal like a seed exiting its pod.

"I'll do it anyway," Corinne whispered through clenched teeth. "You can't stop me! I won't let you snitch to the Children's Council!"

But she knew it was an idle threat. As long as the baby resided inside their mother, they could only communicate with her. But once out, even though helpless and floppy for some time, the newborn could use their brain to talk to other children who ruled the village. The capacity for brain-to-brain communication waned as the child grew up, along with intelligence, and disappeared around the age of seven, after which a member of the Children's Council was retired.

Corinne hobbled inside and lay on her bed—a pallet of woven twigs. The flowers growing on the ceiling dipped down their white, pink and yellow crowns, their eyespots observing her closely.

"Fuck you!" she muttered as one of them, a lush Rosea, emitted a puff of nauseatingly sweet scent supposed to calm her down. It did make her feel somewhat disconnected from her body, which was a blessing.

Pain came in regular waves, and she rode them, clinging to her defiance like a drowning man to a wooden plank. There was an actual plank clutched in her hand.

Dead wood: a piece of somebody's mother, brother, or lover.

Edward came in but she shooed him out. She did not want him to see her like this. His memory of his own birth was quite different: chatting to her as he crawled through the scarlet tunnel of the birth canal toward light. It had been easy. Corinne had not fought against him as she was fighting against her daughter. The girl refused to communicate as she grimly pushed her way out of Corinne's body. She knew why the girl wanted to be born now.

"You bloody tattletale," she whispered with cracked lips, and was rewarded with another wave of pain.

The girl would tell on her immediately after birth, and, free of her fleshy incubator, would watch with undoubted satisfaction as Corinne and probably Edward would be escorted by the cowed adults to the boundary of the village, while babies sat in judgment. And then they would have to make their way through the dense thicket of carnivorous trees, whose scarlet-veined pitchers filled with acid would open like hungry mouths at the approach of such a substantial meal. Nobody knew what lay beyond the forest of pitcher trees because nobody had gone this way for decades.

Throughout her labor, Corinne did not cry out. But now a hoarse scream was torn out of her, as with one last wrenching muscle contraction, she expelled the intruder.

Edward rushed in when he heard her cry and looked over her shoulder at his sister.

Until now, her daughter had only been only the intrusive censorious voice carried on the tide of her blood into every corner of her body. But now, as Corinne cut the umbilical and wrapped her in a piece of cloth, she was suddenly a baby—a solid little bundle with flailing pink arms and legs. She was tiny, but with a full head of curly black hair.

She opened her eyes and coughed, little bubbles forming on her pink lips. Corinne caught her breath. The girl's eyes were dark blue.

For a moment, mother and daughter contemplated each other, and then the baby spoke. As with all newborns, her speech was somewhat slurred, but Corinne understood.

"The Council knows I was born."

Corinne nodded, her battered and bruised body throbbing. All she wanted now was to close her eyes and sleep.

Her fingers closed over the fireboard she had prepared. When the Council members came, they would see it immediately. But Corinne did not have the strength to try to hide it. Anyway, it would be useless. The girl knew about it.

Her eyes, so large in her scrunched-up red face, moved to Edward who nodded awkwardly, clearly not knowing whether he should introduce himself.

"Brother," the girl said and tried to reach out with her splayed hand. She could not: newborns had very poor coordination for the first couple of days after birth. Edward touched her pink fingers and looked pleadingly at Corinne.

"We won't be around her for long, you and I." Corinne said bitterly. "The Council will take care of it."

"I did not tell them," the girl said.

"What?"

"I did not tell them about the fireboard," the girl repeated. "And now you take me to Nana."

***

They walked to the plantation, the three of them: Corinne carrying the baby in a sling, and Edward supporting his mother. A couple of adults looked at them dully, but it was harvest time, and they were busy gathering fruit.

They stood in front of the tree that had been Aliana, and Corinne realized that her mother was gone. The tree was lush and green, its branches heavy with foliage, its bark hardening. A small roundish fruit was beginning to ripen on the tip of a low limb, and the baby reached out to it.

Corinne slapped her hand.

"No!" she said sharply. "That was a human being. Your grandmother."

"But you fed me when I was inside you!"

"Because I had to. But you have a choice now."

The baby turned her blue eyes to her mother and brother.

"If you set fire to the trees," she said in her lisping voice, "what would happen to the village?"

Corinne did not know and did not care. Edward answered instead.

"We will leave this place. Look for a new home. A human place, not a tree plantation."

"But you are no longer what humans used to be!"

Edward shrugged.

"We'll find out, won't we?"

"You will die," the girl said.

"Better die as humans than live as plants."

Corinne, no longer listening, knelt before the Mother Tree and started rubbing the dry stick in the notch of the fireboard like it was shown in the book. Her head swam with exertion. A trickle of blood crawled down her thigh.

Brother and sister whispered to each other. And then the girl addressed her.

"I could still talk to the Council."

"I know you can." Corinne's palms were sweaty, but she was beginning to see a tiny curl of smoke rising from the pile of dry moss.

"But I won't if you take me with you."

"What?" Corinne almost dropped the stick.

"Yes!" Edward interjected. "She wants to come with us. It's OK, mum. I can carry her."

"But..." And then Corinne understood.

She looked at her daughter and saw the woman she would grow into if she stayed in Peony: the woman pollinated by predatory flowers; forced to carry babies who would control her like a beast of burden; fated to lose bits and pieces of her mind, watching her humanity fade as nature subsumed her into its endless uncaring cycle. The woman who would become a tree.

The curl of smoke grew into a plume, and the acrid smell of burning cut through the sweetness of blooming trees and flowers. Corinne spread the flaming moss around the base of the tree and saw a worm of fire climb toward its crown.

She picked up her daughter and walked toward the pitcher-tree forest. Before following, Edward rushed back to the tree and picked a smoldering branch. The baby whimpered, and Corinne, with a sigh, unbuttoned her dress and pushed a nipple into her mouth.

"What's my sister's name?" Edward asked.

"Aliana," Corinne said. "Her name is Aliana."

Live Oak

Carly Racklin

Carly Racklin is a writer, editor, and bird enthusiast currently nesting in the mountains of Tennessee. Her fiction has appeared in Metaphorosis Magazine, The NoSleep Podcast, Frozen Wavelets, and more. You can find more of her work at carlyracklin.com, and follow her on Twitter @willowylungs.

The tree looked like it had lost a fight. A bad one—the kicking, squealing, bloody kind from the movies that played after dark. It didn't seem like it should still be standing, but it was, clinging to the dirt with scraggly roots like fingers snapped at every joint.

A pinkish scar ran down the thickest part of the trunk, and an entire limb was missing, with just a jagged stump left over. The rest of its branches stretched out at crooked, uncomfortable angles, though together they still reached taller than the very top of our new two-story house. Its sharp shadow covered me and half the lawn and ran up the walls to the gray shingle roof.

"That's the ugliest tree I've ever seen," Finn said, flopping onto his back in the grass beside me.

A breeze rushed by and we both sighed as it cooled the sweat on our skin. It was a cloudless, angrily hot day, and we'd maybe gotten three good breezes in the entire afternoon we spent carrying all the boxes in from the moving truck. I'd been out of breath for hours.

From underneath, the tree looked unbalanced, and staring at it made me feel like I was on the edge of falling over too. "Something's wrong with it," I said. A little wall of stones circled the trunk: a barricade to keep something out, or maybe in.

Finn snickered. "Dare you to touch it."

Green splotches speckled most of the bark. My ears burned, already hearing how Finn would laugh if I chickened out. I wiped my clammy palms on my shorts and reached for the tree.

Just before my hand could touch the trunk, Finn kicked the back of my leg. I folded over forward, arms pinwheeling. My cheek scraped the knobbly bark as I hugged the trunk for balance. When my breath caught up to me, I yelped and peeled myself away. The green spots stuck to my skin. I choked back a gag.

Eventually Finn stood and brushed his palm over the same spot. "Weird," he scoffed, grimacing, then wiped his hand down the back of my shirt.

"Finneas, Rory, come inside," Mom yelled from the doorway, her dark brown arms glistening and folded tight against her chest. She was too late to notice anything, like always. "First one in picks their room!"

Finn made it up the drooping porch steps in a blur, while I couldn't move an inch. My skin felt wrong, dry and slick at the same time. I double- and triple-checked, but even though there weren't any bugs, I couldn't shake off the feeling of something crawling on me.

Stiff at the joints like one of my dolls waiting to be unpacked, I walked silently inside, and didn't look back.

I shivered all through my first shower in the new house. The water that puddled under my feet ran a pale, sickly green.

Finn picked the bigger room, so I got the one at the front of the house, with a wide window looking right out at the yard. As I stuffed my drawers full of clothes, the tree's branches swayed at the edges of my vision. I didn't have curtains to close yet.

It was terrible, the same kind of terrible as when Finn put on that Blair Witch movie when Mom and Dad were out one night. I couldn't stop watching.

But this time was different. Worse. I felt it watching me back.

***

That night the tree came for me.

I woke up to its shadow stretched across my bed like a giant hand. I screamed, scrambling out of my blankets and up against the wall. But there was nowhere to go. The branches snatched at my feet.

Mom slammed open my door, and by the time I'd blinked the shadows had let go. In the dim light, the bags under her eyes looked like deep holes. She must've been awake already to have come running so quick. The silk scarf around her hair shimmered with moonlight as she sat beside me and took my face in her hands. Fear kept me pinned flat to the wall.

"I knew it, I knew it was bad." My mouth was dry, like I'd been talking in my sleep again.

"Oh, honey," Mom whispered, trying to wrap me in a hug. She smoothed her cold fingers over the hand-me-down scarf around my own hair. "It was just a nightmare. You're not used to the house yet."

Maybe she was right. But it wasn't the house that tried to take me.

After I quieted down, Mom kissed me on both cheeks and slipped out of the room.

I moved my bed that night, slowly, quietly, and with nobody's help. I pushed until my arms ached and the side pressed flat against the opposite wall, farthest from the window. But I didn't sleep.

Every night since then, I'd woken up to see that crooked shadow creeping across the floor toward me. I felt it watching, waiting for something too awful to name. Something cold like Dad's eyes and dark like Mom's, awful like the glares they shared from across the dinner table or in the front seats of the car when they thought Finn and I couldn't see. But we always saw. And now, it saw too.

We moved in on the last day of June. By the middle of July I knew the tree was haunted. Knew it deep down in the dark place in my belly where every ugly feeling lived.

But knowing wasn't going to be enough.

***

After a month, we stopped at the library to get our cards. At the front desk, a wrinkled white woman in too-bright lipstick took down our information, asking enough questions to make my head spin. When Mom mentioned the house and Dad's job that made us move, the lady's eyes lit up. She nodded like she knew all about it, like building and tearing things down was a big deal.

Eventually I stopped listening and walked up and down the aisles of books, trailing my fingers over the different lumpy spines. The old ones were the best, always so soft.

I circled around one shelf and almost bumped into a tall goth girl with box braids and rings on every finger. Her name tag said Mallory.

"Are those heavy?" I asked. She must have had strong hands.

She narrowed her eyes, ringed with smudged black pencil. Maybe she was training for some kind of hand weight-lifting contest. Maybe that was what people did for fun in big empty towns with no sidewalks, where random librarians knew who your dad was because there's only one construction company for miles.

I took a deep breath. "Do you have books about trees?"

She cocked her hip, smacking the cart of books beside her. It rattled like it was a hundred years old. "Um, yeah," she said. "They're right over—"

"What about haunted trees?" The words came out like a scream even though I tried to whisper them. No matter what you did in libraries, it always sounded too loud.

Mallory stared, and my ears got so hot I thought they would melt down the sides of my head like candle wax. But she didn't make a face, or call me weird—she smiled, and said, "Yeah. We have some books like that. Follow me."

Mallory looked like people asked her weird things a lot.

When I came back, Mom was still talking to the woman at the front desk, her lips twitching to stay stretched in their friendly smile. Finn looked bored enough to fall asleep right on the vomit-colored carpet.

"Well now, you've been busy," the woman said when I handed over the stack of books. Her eyes flicked over them, then up at Mom.

Mom stared too, but I could tell she didn't want to seem embarrassed in front of this librarian who apparently knew all about us, because she nodded and said, "Oh, yes. Rory has a very mature taste in books. She loves to read."

The woman smiled back. She had lipstick on her teeth. "Of course," she said, and scanned all the books, passing each one to me afterward.

I grinned the whole way back to the car, my arms shaking under the books' weight. On the ride home, Finn read the titles out over my shoulder. *The Willows. The Ritual. The Pines. The Girl Who Loved Tom Gordon. The Hazel Wood.*

With each one, his voice got more and more of that nasally tone he always used whenever he called me weird, though I knew he wouldn't say it in front of Mom. He'd do it once we were home, when Mom and Dad argued or worked or went out on one of their "dates." But I didn't care.

For the first time in weeks, I felt something like safe.

***

I looked up from *The Girl Who Loved Tom Gordon* and out over the porch when I saw it. A spot, not quite white, standing out against the dirt under the tree. I blinked. The tree creaked.

Five minutes later it was still there. I kept reading the same sentence again and again, but none of the words sunk in. Every time I glanced up at the tree, that odd little speck stared back.

It's for me.

As soon as I thought it, the dark place in my belly roared and a surge of nausea bowled me over. I closed the book.

It took me five more minutes to shuffle off the porch and slink through the dry grass of the yard. The yellowing blades tickled my ankles.

A tiny figurine sat nestled between the knobs of the tree's trunk. Without breathing I reached over the stone wall and snatched it up.

It just barely fit in the palm of my hand. The longer I traced its slight curves with my fingertips, the more familiar it felt: hand-made, like my dolls. Not totally smooth but not sloppy either. I couldn't tell if it had been painted at some point, or if it was just dirty.

Something creaked again. I looked up. A big black crow perched on one of the branches. Another joined it, and another, until there were no empty branches left. They cawed to each other in secret, sharp voices. The kind Mom and Dad used when they fought after Finneas and I were supposed to be in bed.

All at once, the crows flapped into the air and dove at me.

I screamed, dropping to the ground and covering my head until the noise stopped. When I opened my eyes, it was just me and the tree again.

I glared, itchy all over, but not from the grass. Dad liked to say that if you didn't stand up to bullies, you let them win. Of course, when you were the smaller one, it wasn't that easy. But I doubt Dad had ever been the smaller one in a fight.

"Leave me alone," I said, pushing myself up and brushing off my legs. "I'm not afraid of you." Could haunted things tell if you lied to them, like parents could? I hoped not.

The tree swayed. A crow squawked in the sky.

I wrapped both hands around the little statue and ran inside.

***

"Maybe it's a charm. Or one of those Catholic saint statues?" Mom said at the other end of the dinner table, holding the figurine between two fingers.

"Hmm. Looks like a chess piece to me. Where did you find it?" Dad asked.

"Under the tree. It wasn't there yesterday."

"Maybe the previous owners buried it. It could be an antique," said Mom.

I stabbed a pea with my fork and it broke open with a wet pop. "Can we cut it down?"

"Cut it down? Of course not! It's a beautiful tree," Dad's furry blond eyebrows lowered over his eyes. "Trees are good things, Rory. They help us breathe, you know."

"I know. What about all the trees you cut down for work?"

Dad's fork wavered on the way to his mouth. "What about them?"

"Aren't they beautiful too?"

Mom's knife screeched across her plate.

"It would crash right into my room if it fell. It's big enough," I said. "Trees fall all the time."

"And since when did you become an arborist?" asked Dad. Redness had started to bloom on his freckled cheeks, and I knew better than to keep pressing.

I took a sip of water. My hand shook around the glass. "I've been reading a lot."

Mom passed the carved figure back over to me. "You and that tree are just going to have to learn to get along, Rory." Her voice was sludgy like the gravy oozing over her plate.

She'd said the exact same thing about me and Finn. And he'd been kicking me under the table since I was big enough to sit in a chair.

Out of the dining room window, though the sun had set, I could still make out the black shape of the trunk. It always looked angrier in the dark.

That night, I put the figurine on the shelf with all my dolls, right in the center. I kept my curtains open.

I dreamt of axes.

***

I woke up standing under the tree in almost pitch darkness. The wind rushed like tidal waves in my ears. The statue was back in the circle of stones. I tried to yell, but my voice sounded washed away. My teeth chattered so hard they ached. The tree's bony limbs rocked heavily back and forth.

I'm not afraid of you. I'm not afraid of you, I thought. Maybe, if I told myself enough, it would start to be true.

I reached for the statue, but strong arms wrapped around my shoulders.

"Rory—what the *hell*—what are you doing out here? It's the middle of the night! There's a storm coming!" It was Dad's voice, but I didn't see him, I just kept reaching. He threw me up over his shoulder and stomped across the lawn. I kicked and squirmed all the way back to the house.

The door slammed shut, but I didn't feel safe. Not anymore.

Dad let me down; I landed funny on one ankle and yelped. For a minute he didn't say anything, just huffed in the skewed half-light of the hall. The shadows warped his face into a frowning mask, his white skin turned so pasty he looked dead.

"You get back to bed, Rory."

Now I couldn't keep the words down. "But—the tree—it took—"

"*Go!*"

I shut up, and hobbled upstairs.

I sat awake for the rest of the night. The tree waved as the rain came down, the lightning making it glow like a hand with all the skin shredded off.

***

I returned the books. In the library, Mallory was reading a story to some kids in a corner painted too bright to look at for long. She stood out against the walls, her black lipstick almost the same shade as her skin. I sat down and watched through squinted eyes.

She waved around her ringed hands and did voices for every character. All the words sounded bright and true when she read them.

I almost dozed off in my chair, but sat up when I heard the clacking of the buckles on Mallory's boots come closer. Her braids, too many to count, fell in shimmering sweeps across her shoulders as she passed.

"Hey," she said, waving.

"Those books didn't work."

Mallory stopped, and turned back to me. I kept my eyes on her shiny boots, worried I'd start tearing up. "What do you mean they didn't work?"

"I read them and they didn't do anything. They didn't help at all." I fought back a yawn. I hadn't slept through the night in weeks. "It's only getting worse."

She walked over slowly; I could hear the deep frown in her voice. "What's getting worse?"

I shrugged. "Everything."

Around us, the library seemed even quieter than usual. Eerie and empty and a little too cold.

"Hey," Mallory said in a low murmur, "follow me."

"What?"

"Just—come on." She glanced around, then marched off through the shelves and toward the back of the library. My head spun as I stood, but I caught up with her.

Somehow, Mallory walked the same way she read stories. Not like a contest to prove she was good at it, but like it mattered.

When we reached the wall, she opened a tall gray door and waved me in. Inside was a little room with plush leather chairs, a table, and the tiniest refrigerator I'd ever seen. She opened it and took out a plastic baggie.

"You like carrots?"

"Um. Yeah?"

"Sweet." She sat down on one of the chairs and opened the bag. "Go ahead." She pointed to the chair next to her. I sat. She handed me a tiny carrot stick. It was cold and damp.

"Thanks." I popped the whole thing into my mouth and chewed.

"So why do you need books on haunted trees?"

The carrot got stuck in my throat on the way down. Mallory noticed, because in the next second she reached back into the refrigerator and pulled out a water bottle, also tiny. I took a few sips. The water slithered down into my belly with all the other cold things. "Promise you won't laugh? Or—call me weird?"

"Promise. Plus, I like weird." She wiggled her fingers. "Weird is cool."

Weird is cool.

"Okay."

So I told her about the tree, and my dreams, and the figurine, and everything.

When I was done, Mallory balled up the plastic baggie and threw it into a garbage can across the room. I forced down the last carrot. At least Mom couldn't be mad that I spoiled my dinner if it was with vegetables.

"Why do you think it's the tree?" she asked finally. She'd been quiet, fiddling with her rings for so long I couldn't tell if she planned to say anything at all. "I've never heard of a haunted tree before, but I've heard of a lot of haunted houses."

I took another long drink of water, remembering the shadows, and the itchiness on my skin, and that awful, teetering feeling. "I have a brother. I know what it feels like when someone's trying to torment me." That's what Mom called it sometimes, when Finn did his worst. But Finn always got bored eventually.

I didn't even want to think about where this might end, what would happen when I was finally too tired to fight it. "It won't leave me alone. It even made me sleepwalk after I took that doll."

"Why show you the doll at all, then? Maybe it wanted you to have it."

"It made me give it back."

"Or something else did." She looked up, eyes bright but far away. "What's your new house like?"

"I don't know—old. What does it matter? It's the tree that's bad, not the house. You're not listening."

Mallory hunched over her knees and squinted. "Wait—hold on. Let me think. It just doesn't add up."

My whole face burned. I stood. "I have to go."

I pushed the door open and ran, past all the books and out the front of the library. I sat on a bench and waited for Mom to come back from her errands. By the time she pulled up to the curb, I had finished crying, and Mallory hadn't come looking for me.

***

That night I listened to Mom and Dad shouting through the floor, my ear pressed flat against the wood. They weren't even trying to be quiet this time.

When I crossed the hall to go to the bathroom, Finn stood on the landing, his hands shaking around the bars of the railing. The angry lines of his face stood out even in the dark. He had a funny look in his eyes, almost like the one he usually gave me before doing something he knew he wasn't allowed to, just to see what would happen.

The muscles in his arms clenched and unclenched; white spots bloomed and faded on his knuckles. I watched for a while, and then I figured it out. He was thinking about jumping off.

I shivered all over, and one of the old floorboards creaked under me. Finn whipped around, then bolted back into his room and slammed the door. The frame rattled like an earthquake had rolled through.

The voices downstairs finally stopped.

***

A letter came from Mallory a few days later.

"Hey. I'm sorry about the other day.

Linda at the front desk told me you're the ones that moved into the Lark house. I had no idea. I've been trying to get the mayor to tear that place down for a year, but he calls it historic.

The Larks built that house back around the Civil War. They were slave owners, as bad as it gets. And that tree has been around since before anyone ever built on the land. It's probably older than the whole town.

Listen. It's not that tree you need to worry about. I don't think nature can be bad like that. I think those bad feelings you have are from the house. It shouldn't even be on the map, let alone have that family's name still attached to it.

I'm sorry for not listening before. I don't know if you have a phone but I wrote down my number just in case. Come by the library anytime if you want to talk. I can show you some more books you might like.

Be careful."

My stomach twisted in knots.

Dad must have known about the Larks when he bought the house. He was the boss of his company, which meant he was important, and important people had to know important things like that. But Mom—who looked like she was getting even less sleep than me—would never have agreed to let us move here if she knew the whole story. Dread and anger buzzed through my spine, and I wanted to crush the paper in my hands.

An old picture was folded into the envelope along with the letter. It was of the house, with the tree a familiar sharp jumble in the foreground. A white family stood in front of it: a husband and wife, and three kids sitting lined up on one of the low branches.

I peeked out the window. That branch was missing now.

***

The next day I found one of my dolls in pieces on my bedroom floor.

I cut my fingers trying to pick up the shards of its body, too stunned to cry. It was the one Mom had gotten made to look just like me for my thirteenth birthday. She'd said it would be my last one, since I wasn't a little girl anymore.

I held its bristly mop of hair to my chest, glaring out the window, and finally cried harder than I had in weeks.

Finn got the worst scolding of his life that night. He said again and again that he didn't do it, and I did too, when I could talk again.

Dad ignored us both. Mom hugged me in my room after sweeping up the pieces and said I shouldn't try to keep Finn out of trouble just because I felt bad.

"But it's not his fault," I croaked.

"I know," Mom said. She held me tighter, and we both tried not to hear the yelling from downstairs.

***

The next time I dreamed, I dreamed of my room.

Everything moved like wet paint, all sloppy and blue. I nudged the window open. The breeze brushed over me, cool and quiet, too calm to be real while I was still so twisted up inside.

Deep breaths. In, out.

If I could just breathe more of it in, maybe it would help. I stuck out my head, but it still wasn't enough, so I climbed out onto the windowsill. I balanced my feet on it and leaned my whole body out, clutching the inside of the glass.

I stretched one of my arms out, and the wind whistled between my fingers and over my skin like a ghost's breath. My T-shirt whipped against my stomach. I breathed in as deep as I could, but only felt emptier.

The tree watched me from the middle of the yard, brighter than the big half-moon up in the sky. It rocked in the wind like it was trying to climb out of the ground.

Cold fingers wriggled under my own and loosened my grip. I slipped in slow motion, turning back to the window, expecting to find Finn's sneering face behind the glass before I cried myself awake.

There was no one there but my own screaming reflection.

***

I blinked at the grass, the scream still raw in my throat. My arms dangled below me, reaching, but not touching the ground. All I heard was my thrashing heart.

My head felt like a balloon about to pop. The longer I stared at the blurry grass, the more nauseous I felt, so I pressed my chin down against my collarbone, and saw the sky.

Crooked branches had my ankles in a vice grip. I followed them with my eyes, and even though everything was topsy-turvy and my vision was fuzzy from all the blood pooling down, I saw the tree.

A web of roots had burst partly out of the dirt. The rest of it was in a tangled slant, reaching across the yard to my open bedroom window.

If I was right-side-up, I would have screamed some more, I thought. Or thrown up. But then the tree lurched, its limbs groaning low, and I watched our shadows fly together across the lawn. There was nothing to hold on to.

I whimpered in a paper-thin voice, "Don't let go, don't let go, please—"

More creaks, and the ground closed in, until my palms pressed flat against dirt. The branches unhooked, leaving me in a handstand, before I fell in a heap in the circle of stones. All the blood rushed back through me.

Instead of getting sick, I flopped on my side against the tree's gnarled trunk and fainted.

***

"What did you *do?*"

I woke up to Finn kneeling over me, his face like a crumpled piece of paper.

"What did you do?" he repeated. The sun was just barely rising over his shoulder, outlining his hair in a fiery halo. I blinked and sat up.

The dull figurine fell out of my hands.

I ignored Finn, and twisted around to look at the tree. The ground by its trunk was lumpy; some of its roots still peeked out of the dirt.

When I turned back, Finn wiped at his eyes with the side of one tight fist. "Get back inside, Rory. Before Mom and Dad find you."

I swallowed down a hard lump. "Something's wrong."

"I know." He grabbed handfuls of my shirt and started to heave me up, but I put my hands over his and planted my feet down hard. He'd have to drag me or listen.

"No." I shook my head. "I mean *here.* It's worse now. It's not just us."

"Rory, come *on.*"

My toes dug into the dirt, fighting his weight. "I know you know it too. It's—weird, right?"

"Making up stories won't make it go away."

"Neither will hurting yourself. Or thinking about it."

Finn grimaced like I'd slapped him. He shoved me back. I stumbled into the tree, and a section of its bark flaked off with a soft crunch. "What's wrong with you? I'm not the one who just jumped out of my window!"

"It wasn't me!" I answered in a whisper-shout. "It wasn't my idea. Just like it wasn't you who broke my doll."

He didn't say anything for a minute, but stood far away from me, his eyes fixed on the dirt.

"Why can't you just deal with things in the real world, like everybody else?"

My throat burned. "*I am*. It's not my fault no one will listen." Tears bubbled up in me, and my lower lip trembled. "I bet even if nothing caught me when I jumped you still wouldn't believe me. You just want to be angry. But we have to do something."

Finn kept looking down, blinking again and again. "We can't, Rory," he mumbled. "It's already over."

I pressed my hand to the trunk, fingers grazing the green puzzle-piece shapes on its bark. In the sunrise, we had the same warm brown skin. "No—we can't. But it can. It has been, for a long time, I think."

His brows came down over his eyes. He shook his head. "That's just a tree. It can't help us! It can't change anything!"

He didn't know that it had just saved my life.

"Nothing here is *just* anything. It's not just a tree. And that's not just a house. And we're not just a normal, happy family." I sucked in a thin breath. "Don't bother trying to lie to me about that."

Finn shook his head again, slower this time, and in the light his eyes were wet and shiny too. "Mom and Dad are getting a divorce."

I breathed but the air didn't come. It stopped somewhere in my throat and dug in all its claws.

"What?"

"I saw the papers in their room." He reached for me, but I shook him off. "It's already done, Rory."

"Shut up. Stop lying." The tears dribbled down and wouldn't stop.

He reached again, and this time grabbed me by the shoulders. I tried to move out of the way but stumbled on a root and tripped into his chest. I wrapped my arms around his middle for balance and hung on. His heartbeat boomed like a thunderstorm.

"Let's go inside," Finn said. I barely heard him. I nodded against his shirt.

But we didn't go. We just held on.

***

I slept cradling the little statue, with not a single nightmare. By the time I woke up again it was past noon and Mom and Dad were gone. I pawed through every drawer I could find but there were no divorce papers anywhere. Finn wouldn't come out of his room.

In the kitchen, I pulled out Mallory's letter and dialed the number. Thunder rumbled outside, shaking the window frames.

A staticky voice answered, "Hello?"

"Mallory?"

There was a long pause. "Rory?"

"Yeah."

"Hey." I heard shuffling in the background. "How are you? Is everything okay?"

I tangled my fingers in the curly phone wire and paced, following the loops of the wood boards in the floor. I wondered how many trees had died to make them. "I think you were right. Something happened. With the tree—and the house."

Rain pelted the windows.

"What happened? Are you okay?"

"I'm fine. I sleepwalked again. Or...sleep-jumped. Out of my window."

The garbled static swallowed most of Mallory's swear.

"Rory, listen to me," she said. "It's not safe in that house."

"I'm okay now, really," I tried to talk louder over the noise. "The tree saved me."

"*What?*"

I pressed the phone harder against my ear. Thunder boomed again, and the lights flickered. "Mallory? Are you there?"

A short burst of broken syllables came through the receiver, then the line went dead.

I dropped the phone back into its cradle on the wall. Above my head, the floor shook.

"Finn?" No answer.

I plodded up the stairs. Down the hall, framed in the window of my room, Finn stood in shadow. I ran in, my heart ricocheting around in my chest.

As soon as I stepped inside, the shape of him melted into the floor. The door slammed shut behind me before I'd finished gasping.

I screamed. First for nothing, then for Finn. The doorknob wouldn't budge.

"Rory?" his muffled voice answered after a few seconds. Then again, closer, "Rory, what's going on?"

I banged my fists on the painted wood. "It won't open!" He didn't reply, but the door rattled some more. I tried the window next, but it stayed down like it'd been glued shut. Outside, the tree's branches bent wildly in the wind. Its roots inched further out of the ground with every gust.

All the lights flickered out. Finn's footsteps moved away into silence, then came back after what felt like hours.

"Rory, all the doors and windows are locked. I can't open them. The phone doesn't work," he cried, beating harder on the door.

I flattened myself against the wall just as my shelf tipped over. It hit the ground with a hundred tiny crashes.

I couldn't scream anymore, could barely breathe. I watched the tree outside the window, my eyes burning and watering from trying not to blink. The world blurred into nothing but a gray soup, the clouds so dark it could've been dusk.

Glass shattered downstairs.

I gasped, and blinked stinging tears down my cheeks. Then I could make out the silvery car-shape parked diagonally in our driveway, its door flung open and headlights cutting yellow streaks across the lawn.

Mallory's voice broke through the storm's ruckus. She shouted my name, clear and blaring. It was her storytelling voice.

For a second I thought it was just another trick. Then she hollered from right outside, with Finn an echo behind her, "Rory, get away from the door."

I slid my feet along the floor, pushing aside pieces of my dolls' porcelain faces. The figurine was lost in the puzzle of their splintered parts. "Okay," I called back.

Lightning painted the whole world white.

Thunder rattled again and again, so loud I thought the house was exploding, but then my door cracked off its hinges, and Mallory's tall dark shape rushed in.

She crushed me in a hug, and I finally breathed again. She smelled like coffee and books, the old, soft kind. The best kind. Finn grabbed my arm like he meant to break it, though his hands trembled.

"Everybody out, *now*." Mallory grabbed my other arm, and we all bolted across the landing. Halfway down the stairs I stumbled and my ankle screamed with pain. Before I missed a beat, Finn threw my arm over his shoulder and helped me the rest of the way down, though his face was twisted up in pain. When we reached the bottom, he limped too.

The big window in the dining room was broken open.

Mallory kicked aside shards of glass, and smoothed her leather jacket over the window sill. Blood dripped down one leg of her torn jeans. She half-shoved, half-lifted me out onto the porch.

Finn tumbled out next. Mallory climbed through and crouched beside us when lightning struck the tree.

The ground really did shake then, and the bottom of the trunk crackled, splintered, and exploded into bright slivers.

We all watched and felt the rumble fade. But the splintering sound didn't stop. The tree teetered for a second, then tipped.

Mallory grabbed Finn and me by our closest limbs and scrambled off the porch. Gravel slashed my feet as we hit the driveway. I whined with each step, still watching as the tree lurched parallel to us, and crashed through the middle of the roof. Right into my bedroom.

"*Holy shit,*" Mallory coughed, still clutching us both. A wave of relief cooled her voice.

Rain soaked me through, cold, like the summer was finally gone. I swiped the sopping hair from my eyes.

The bottom of the trunk sputtered and smoked, a gaping hole in its side.

With its beams jutting out like broken and crushed bones, our house groaned around its wound—a long, final sigh.

Of Wood and Flame

Anna Madden

Anna Madden lives in North Texas, where the prairie reaches long tallgrass fingers toward the woods. Her fiction has appeared in Hexagon, Zooscape, Orion's Belt, Medusa Tales, PodCastle, Metaphorosis, and elsewhere. She has an English degree from the University of Missouri—Kansas City. In free time she gardens, mountain bikes, and makes birch forests out of stained glass. Follow her on Twitter @anna_madden_ or visit her website at annamadden.com.

Fossil—oldest of the Yromem—had survived many seasons. He had known blight, powdery mildew, cedar rusts, drought, and more. His ancient roots burrowed to unknown depths. Still, when Fossil looked upon Holly, she noticed his leaves twitched. His thoughts seemed hard to gather, much less voice. Even so, he spoke.

"Give that furless cub back to her own kind," Fossil said. "Or better yet, leave her to wither and die."

Standing in Longleaf's shade, Holly clenched a string of flint around her neck and stared at Fossil. Took in his rough bark, his crooked joints. His voice frightened her, so raspy, with the lingering sting of a wasp.

"Holly is mine," Longleaf said, her summer-green leaves rustling in protest. "A cub is like a seed. It needs the sun. It thirsts and is eager to grow."

"This cub you claim stirs memories of ash and smoke," Fossil said. "She might burn the forest to stumps. She could grow wings and steal the very sky."

His words had a fierce bite. Holly held back a sob until it burned her throat. She turned and fled, running fast through the trees, over fern moss and across narrow animal trails, until she met the river. Its water glinted silver, and its direction was certain. Holly touched the water and felt its chill across her bare skin, for she grew no fur, nor leaves or bark. Her long mane fell forward, hiding her cheeks.

Time passed, and the sun moved with it. A creak of wood sounded, then a canopy of shade fell over Holly. She pushed back her hair and sniffed, taking in a sharp, sweet odor. Longleaf smelled of pine, for her thin leaves were numerous upon her strong branches.

"I first found you among the mayflies and the reeds," Longleaf said. She moved closer, her roots tangled beneath her, snagging in the dirt. "You are like a salmon who returns to the water of its birth."

The river flowed by. Holly envied how it knew where it must go. "Is it true, what Fossil said?"

"His memories are old," Longleaf said. "He fears the dragon who lost its fire and wants it back."

"You said I wouldn't wake him," Holly said. She picked up a stone and threw it into the passing current. "Sleeping Yromem only stir when the winds are strong or before a hard freeze."

"Fossil has stood in one place a long time," Longleaf said. "I don't know why he woke, but words like his have many meanings. Best to leave such things buried, I think, and out of the sunlight."

Holly scrambled to her feet and wrapped her arms around Longleaf's trunk. "Am I a wolf without fur, then? If I were, I'd belong here, with you."

"You must choose for yourself," Longleaf said. "Even I must grow roots, then find a place to plant them."

***

The seasons turned. Holly remembered them as a blur of honeysuckle and frost-gilded wood ferns, maple-red leaves and fragile green shoots. She was not meant to recollect but to learn. Holly tried to keep her face in the sun's warmth. To never turn bitter or gnarled inside.

Her nails grew. Her smooth skin, once paler than sunlight, deepened to the color of ripe acorns. She took to adding a layer of thick mud to her cheeks, to her would-be trunk, and the strands of her dark mane. She stuck fallen leaves to the wet dirt across her skin. When it dried, it left a rough texture similar to ash-brown bark. Holly learned to avoid sumac leaves, locust thorns, and sick-making mushrooms. She read the tracks of rabbits and stalked wolves, and she evaded old roots lest they trip her.

Sometimes saplings asked to see her fire, crowding her, their stem-thin branches pointing to the flint swinging around her neck. Holly created sparks for them.

"You shouldn't do that," Longleaf said when she heard of it. Her words harsh and cold as a winter gale.

Holly clenched the flint until her fingers turned white. "I've had it since you found me. I remember that much."

"That bit of rock holds your truths," Longleaf said, "but if you would live among us, you mustn't make fire."

***

In time, Holly learned all Yromem buried their roots. It was a matter of great discussion. There were coveted areas near the meadow, but also rocky soil and full shade to avoid.

"What about at the forest's center, near the river?" Holly asked.

"Not there," Longleaf said. "No one roots so close to Fossil. It's forbidden."

Holly tilted her head. What did Fossil protect, to keep others from old-growth and damp leaf litter? She set her jaw. Maybe it was the place she belonged to.

Alone, Holly trekked the woods, her feet arrowed toward the deepest shadows. Her soles were hard underneath and carried her without pain. The ground sloped downward, muddy and twig-covered. She walked among elderly Yromem who slumbered season after season, their great trunks and heavy branches full of golden light. Their wood creaked but none stirred. It was rare for sleeping Yromem to wake.

Holly reminded herself of the fact as she snuck past Fossil, grateful for her smaller size, traveling wide to avoid his roots, stepping over his chosen earth bed with care. As she moved, she didn't dare breathe.

His leaves shivered. Holly paused with one foot suspended. Fossil mumbled. She hurried ahead.

Sunlight flickered through the green brush, highlighting large boulders half-buried in the soil. No Yromem slept here. The space was too narrow between stone and dirt, but there were many smaller ferns with delicate, curled growth, elusive short-leafed ginseng, and spurts of lush hawkweed.

She found a cave. A great, yawning mouth of rock. Hot air blew out of it and swept back her muddy hair, and it made her nose wrinkle, for it smelled of rotten meat.

Holly crept closer. Her feet were deft, and she moved as a wolf on the hunt—alert, with the softest footfalls. The outer rocks held long white scars. She breathed through her mouth to avoid the horrible stench that polluted the air. The sun didn't follow her. In the weak light, Holly looked into the cavern but made out little. She tiptoed forward. Her feet brushed against moss and dampness, and she tripped over a huge root.

A root? Holly bent her knees and held her hands out. What she felt was scaly and warm. It was alive, for it shifted beneath her palms. Holly jumped back. A roar like cracking stone met her ears.

She ran. Fossil yelled as Holly breezed past, but she didn't stop until her feet touched the river. There she waded in the shallows until her heart slowed. She listened hard, but there was nothing save the quiet of the water. She was safe, she told herself. She had not been chased, though her thoughts were dark and scattered.

Like her, what dwelled in the cave was no Yromem.

***

Another season passed. Longleaf sought a permanent spot for her tangled roots. It was a difficult task. The forest floor had grown thick of late, and the brush tall.

Holly rubbed her chin, displacing mud. "There's an old wolf den close by," she said to Longleaf. "Maybe there."

Longleaf followed, her hairy roots dragging behind. Holly led the Yromem near the river's banks, close to encroaching boulders, but not too close to Fossil or the cave. That place, she decided, belonged to fear.

Something white peeked through the greenery and caught her attention. Holly bent and pulled back dark-veined leaves. A wolf glared back at her. She froze. Her sight took in furless bone, and she exhaled. Reaching out, she picked up a wolf's skull. The bottom jaw chattered loose and fell back to the earth. She lifted the rest to her face, then turned to stare at Longleaf through the empty eye sockets.

"I see as a wolf sees," Holly said. She peeled back her lips and showed off her pointy fangs.

"It is good to see as others do," Longleaf said, "but that is not why we came here."

Holly nodded, hiding her disappointment. She'd hoped Longleaf would change her mind. That this season would be no different than the others.

Longleaf circled the small clearing. Her roots twined about each other, tangling. As Holly watched, she imagined aged ridges marked her own too-smooth skin, and that her arms were of wood and leaf.

"I wonder what clouds feel like," Holly said, looking through the skull's empty sockets and eyeing wisps of white in the vault of pale sky.

"I don't know," Longleaf said, for though her branches reached high, they weren't the same as wings.

Holly placed the wolf's skull atop her long mane and tied it into place with an obliging vine. The bone pinched against her own forehead, but it made her feel braver having it there. Maybe she could borrow its truths and its memories.

"This is a good place," Longleaf said. Her words were distant. "The earth is rich here. My roots sense water below."

Holly longed to ask what drove Longleaf to this. Why stand still? It was better to chase the wind than to let it find you. It was useless to argue, though. Longleaf would do as other Yromem before her. Holly couldn't understand. Not really. She walked with the Yromem, but she would never have roots of her own.

With her bare hands, Holly dug, letting her muscles take out her frustration. She pulled up thickets and raked the soil. The sun was low when she finished her task. Clay-streaked earth stained the underside of her nails.

Longleaf planted herself and drifted to sleep. Her needle-like leaves pointed toward the sun's great eye. Birds flocked to her massive trunk, and red squirrels explored her branches.

Holly smiled, but her lips wavered. Longleaf's roots were well-protected by a blanket of soil, and her trunk was rigid under beautiful, thick-layered bark. It could never burn easily, so dense and strong as it was, and her arms wrapped around Holly when she climbed into them, cradling her close.

And yet, Holly felt restless. She reached up and felt the grooves in the wolf's skull. She sighed, then reached her hands up high, where clouds drifted.

***

Holly slept until first light. Dawn glinted through fine-tipped needles. Longleaf held her but did not stir or wake.

With a yawn, Holly climbed down and made her way to a fat-bellied boulder near the river. A cavity under the stone held a store of summer-fattened berries. As she dug, a sapling named Spruce approached. His pace was purposeful but slow. His roots had started to grow in, she noticed, forcing him to take greater care. She eyed his handsome rosy bark through her peripherals. Took in his sharp-edged leaves and his lithe, branching arms.

With flared nostrils, Holly faced him so he might admire her wolf skull.

"You don't scare me," Spruce said, his branches swaying with gentle laughter. "You look like a fawn who lost sight of her mother."

She tapped the wolf's bony muzzle. "I'm no deer."

"Come to think of it," Spruce said, "I haven't seen any wolves this season."

Holly wondered at his words. She had not followed the local pack as usual. Not for some time. "I haven't either." She scratched mud-bark off her chin. "Maybe they found easier prey outside the forest."

"Or," Spruce said, "something scared them off."

"Nothing scares a wolf," Holly said. She tilted her head sideways. "Maybe a bigger wolf, but little else." She chewed a handful of sweet berries, then another.

Spruce shifted closer. "My roots are almost mature."

"I'm not a mole," Holly said, throwing a berry at him. "I can't keep digging out holes for Yromem. I helped Longleaf and now she's left me behind for a world of dreams."

"You sound jealous," Spruce said. "You shouldn't be. You keep fire as a servant around your neck."

Holly frowned. "I'd rather have wings than fire. Fossil said I might grow wings. Said I could become a terrible shadow in the sky."

"You avoid him," Spruce said. "Are you scared, then?"

Holly didn't answer. Instead, she did something she shouldn't: she struck her flint. It made sparks which fell to the ground like flakes of melted rock. She noticed Spruce shudder, for much of the ignorance of his youth had been carved away, for he'd seen wood rot and other blights, but he didn't bolt. She held up her flint so he could see it better.

Spruce shook his upper leaves. "Fire is dangerous. It could eat me. You have no wood to burn. Your hands will keep it safe."

"I have a trunk," Holly said, standing tall. "I have four strong limbs. I am like you but also not. If not with you, where do I belong, then?"

"A wolf pack, maybe," Spruce said. "Isn't that why you wear one's skull?"

She dropped her flint back to her neck. "The wolves, then. I'll find them, and I'll hunt alongside them."

"I wish I could run alongside a pack," Spruce said, his voice grown softer.

Holly plucked a green leaf off Spruce and wove the stem into her snarled mane. "I'll take you wherever I go."

She jogged through the forest in a stir of leaves and a crack of dead twigs. Spruce's leaf fluttered in her mane. Her calves burned, but they carried her, and she made her way to the old den where Longleaf slept. Holly placed a flattened palm against the broad trunk. Her hand trailed across the rough bark, then fell back to her side. Her friend slept without rousing in well-earned peace.

Squatting, Holly searched for paw prints near Longleaf's woody ankles. She discovered none though it was the season for pups. The wolves would be hidden somewhere, protecting their young. A cave would suit their purpose best.

A cave like the one she dreaded. A cold sweat broke across her furless skin. She needed strength. If not hers, then borrowed from another. Holly touched a hand to her wolf skull and pulled it down so it covered her face. It wasn't a perfect fit. Her own features were flatter, and her nose wasn't a muzzle. Still, she looked out of those empty eyes, and exhaled.

Holly spun on her heels and scrambled through brush and over moss-covered boulders. She was a wolf—fierce and bold. She carried sleeping fire, didn't she? Even Fossil trembled in her presence despite his seasoned wood. Holly squared her shoulders. She wouldn't fear secrets hidden in the dark.

***

The sunset met Holly at the cave's entrance. It draped the forest in hues of blush and citrus and fire. The rocky chasm appeared as uninviting as before. A good place for a wolf pack to gather. Except another lived there. Its breath smelled the same: of old meat in the hot sun.

Holly approached on silent feet. With her nose close to the ground, she pushed back ferns and checked for signs of passage: paw prints, remnants of kills, or loose fur. All Holly found were dull scents of sage and crushed leaves beneath the rotten air.

There were no tracks. Not even those of a rabbit. Had she come here for the wolves, or to face a truth? Perhaps she meant to challenge the forest, and see if she belonged to it once and for all.

Either way, Holly was tired of being afraid. She picked up hand-sized stones. She threw one against the cave's entrance, then another. It made a clatter, and she heard something echo. A growl or the fall of rock.

"Hello?" Holly called out. "I'm looking for the wolves."

Hot, sour breath choked the air. Holly pinched her nose.

"No wolves here," a voice said, rumbling through the rock. "They left after I said they couldn't have my cave. I recognize your scent. You came this way before."

"By chance," Holly said, her voice gargled. "I snuck by Fossil, then saw a cave I'd never seen before, and then there was this smell—"

A rough chuckle interrupted her. "Is that why you're holding your snout?"

Holly removed her hand fast but couldn't keep her face from wrinkling. The chuckle turned to a laugh, and the ground shook with it.

"What are you, if not a wolf?" Holly asked. "I wish you'd come out of there and show me. It'll be dark soon."

The laugh stopped. "I can't do that."

Holly pictured Longleaf with her newly buried roots. "Are you stuck?" she asked. "I could help. I'm good at digging, but I'm not a mole, so don't call me one."

"It isn't that. I'd scare you."

On instinct, Holly stepped back. Was she so easily startled? She stomped the growth underfoot. "If I was a true wolf, I wouldn't be afraid. If I were an Yromem, I'd have roots, and I wouldn't wander where I shouldn't. I don't know how I should be or what I should want. I don't know what I am."

"You're neither of those," the voice said. "You smell of salt and iron, of men and their dens of stone and timber. I roared before because I thought you'd come to hunt me. That is what your kind do."

Holly sat, flattening a nice patch of hawkweed. She brought her knees to her chest and rubbed off some mud-bark which yet patched her skin.

"You're not happy with what you are?" the voice said.

"It's not that," Holly said. She gripped the string with her flint and twirled it between her fingers. "You tell me what I am, but I still don't know where I belong. I can't see what you see."

A pause. "I used to be dragon, but I lost my fire. I don't know where I belong either. Not anymore."

"I'm sorry," Holly said. She set her chin on her knees. More mud flaked off. The moon's face was visible above. Wispy clouds flocked it. "Can you tell me," she said, "what do clouds feel like?"

Talons tapped against rock. The dragon peeked out of the cave and two star-like eyes blinked at Holly. She held their gaze. The dragon blew air from its snout, and it was so warm, she almost didn't smell the lingering rot.

"You are braver than a wolf," the dragon said. "I will not hide from you." It clambered from its rocky den. It stood taller than a full-grown Yromem, and its scales were shinier than bark. They were smooth and silvery as a maple. Its wings were folded at its sides. Holly longed to see them spread wide.

"I could give you my memories," the dragon said. "I could tell you that clouds are like a cold, wet tongue, but wouldn't you rather decide for yourself?"

Holly stood up. She craned her neck to get a full look at the dragon. The tail was a long vine, but thicker, and the chest broader than the greatest oak. "You mean, I could fly with you?"

"Yes," the dragon said, snaking its face closer to hers. "It would be a first for me too. A new memory is a rare and precious thing. I collect them."

Holly bit her lip. "You collect them…"

She thought about the flint she wore around her neck, and the mud she had smeared across herself. There was the weight of the wolf's skull on her forehead, and the twirl of Spruce's leaf in her mane. They were tangible and meaningful. Dear, precious things.

Timber creaked. "Out of my way," a gnarled and familiar voice said. "I won't allow this."

Fossil appeared. Squinting, Holly saw damaged roots, their ends splintered, their sides caked in loam-colored dirt. Another Yromem followed in his wake. A glint of distinctive red bark caught Holly's eye.

"Spruce?" she said, crossing her arms. "You woke Fossil?"

"I went to ask him what you were," Spruce said. "He said he smelled fire and ripped up his roots. I tried to calm him, but he wouldn't listen."

The dragon shivered and the ground quaked. It lowered its head, as though trying to blend with the rocks and the moss.

"You know Fossil, too, don't you?" Holly asked.

"He took my fire," the dragon said. "Stole it while I slept."

A dragon without fire was no threat to the Yromem. Still, looking at the dragon, Holly felt tears drop between the wolf's skull and her cheeks. The dragon still had talons and teeth. It could have attacked her, she who pretended to be a wolf, but it hadn't.

"Get out of my way, thankless cub," Fossil said. "Longleaf isn't here to stand for you anymore. I will do what I should have done seasons ago."

"I am no cub." Holly positioned herself in front of the dragon, her stance wide, her feet planted into the dirt beneath her. With her chin raised, she bared her teeth at Fossil and imagined them as menacing as thorn-pointed fangs.

Spruce stood tall beside Holly. He held his branches wide.

Holly kept one eye on Fossil, the other on the dragon. She grabbed the string round her neck and showed her flint to the dragon. "With this," she said, "you can get back what was taken from you. You may have it, so long you promise not to burn this forest. It has been a home for me. A place of growth."

The dragon watched her. "I promise."

Fossil groaned. His leaves shook. "I warned Longleaf. You, who make fire, and that dragon, who breathes it. You are too alike."

The dragon could have taken the flint with ease, but it leaned back on its haunches. It waited with the patience of the changing seasons. Holly uncurled her palm. The dragon bent down and carefully gripped the little shard of flint in its sharp teeth. With one gulp, it swallowed it, then turned its long neck to the side. Facing the cave, it took a deep breath and exhaled. A spark hit the rocky surface. The stones sizzled, bright as embers, then dampened.

"I can't remember when I last did that," the dragon said.

Holly sniffed, tentatively, then deeper, for the air had been scorched clean.

Fossil crowded closer. "You're not welcome here."

Roots snapped on rocks, revealing vulnerable green heartwood underneath. He pointed his branches at Holly. Their ends looked sharp. Spruce blocked the larger Yromem with his slim reddish trunk.

Holly placed a hand on Spruce's trunk. "Don't," she said. "I'll go."

Spruce leaned against her touch. "I will bury my roots in this place. I'll wait for your return."

Looking at narrow, rock-strewn ground, she shook her head. "There's no good soil here. When it's your time, go to where Longleaf stands. The dirt is soft still and easy to root." Holly reached for his leaf in her mane and twirled it, the promise it carried unforgotten.

The dragon crouched low and turned its neck, signaling her.

Holly patted Spruce goodbye. With a heave, she climbed the dragon. Its scales weren't much different from ridged bark, and their texture felt similar. She brought a leg over its back and gripped tight.

Holly touched her wolf skull. She didn't rely on its memory of strength anymore. Still, like the flint on its string, it carried truths. She would find more, even as the dragon collected new memories.

The dragon spread its beautiful dusky wings. Holly leaned over its scaly neck. She fit perfectly on its back. Below, the forest shrank. She looked down at Spruce and Fossil. They looked no larger than young shrubs. Her mane floated behind her like reeds underwater, and the wind sung loud in her ears. A howl escaped her throat. The clouds were so dense, without clear lines, and Holly couldn't hold them. She tried, but her fingers fell through the vapor, gathering tiny wet droplets.

The dragon had spoken the truth. No words could capture this feeling. Perhaps that realization wasn't so remarkable. And yet, it was certain.

It was everything.

The Wee Folk

Keira Reynolds

Keira Reynolds is a trans woman, a software developer who dreams of a new career as a writer. She is currently studying Arts and Humanities (Creative Writing) with the Open University. Other than one piece of flash fiction, 'Conspiracy Theory', which is self published on her own blog (https://keirareynolds.com) 'The Wee Folk' is her first published story.

Ailbhe ran, gasping and stumbling, along the narrow track, a staff of ash-wood clutched in her right hand. Briars and thorns snatched at her cloak and lashed at her legs, arms, and face. To either side the alder-woods stretched back from the path into the shadows, dark and threatening. Weaving in and out between the trees, figures clad in green and brown, each about the height of a rat standing on its hind legs, ran alongside her.

Their mocking laughter taunted her. One darted forward and stabbed at her ankle with a small spear, while another loosed a tiny arrow at her face. Ailbhe cried out in pain and fear, pulled her hooded cloak around her face, and ran faster. Their weapons were too small for any one blow to mortally wound her, but they hurt, and sooner or later, if she did not escape, they would cripple or blind her. She choked back a whimper of fear as she tried not to imagine what the wee folk would do to her then. Their small size would not keep them from killing her. But she would take a long time to die.

She reached the banks of a river. To left and right the river wound between banks that were muddy and choked with rushes and willow. She could not escape that way. Straight ahead a small island split the river in two. Did the little folk swim? Ailbhe could not remember. A tiny arrow struck her in the back of the neck and a little spear jabbed her in the calf as she hesitated. With no other choice left to her, she ran into the river.

The river was not deep, and Ailbhe waded most of the way to the island, only having to swim a few strokes at the deepest part in the middle of the channel before pulling herself up onto the island. She turned back to see if she had left the wee folk behind, but they were scampering up trees like demented squirrels, running along branches that hung out over the river, and leaping from there into the branches of the trees that grew on the island. Some were already running around the shore of the island to cut off her escape. She was trapped.

An arrow struck her in the ear, burning like a hornet's sting. Ailbhe cursed, and forced herself to her feet, stumbling forward awkwardly in water-soaked clothing. She pushed her way through the gorse and willow that grew upon the shores of the island. Further in a low hill rose, and the gorse and willow gave way to a stand of silver-barked birch. There was something about the little folk and birch trees. What was it? She struggled to remember. Granny Brónach had taught her something, or had tried to, if only she had listened.

Another spear-thrust to her ankle broke the chain of thought. She seized her staff at one end with both hands and swung it like a flail, trying to mow down the wee folk that tormented her. They leapt aside, laughing. Not once did she land a blow. More arrows stung her face and hands, and more spear-thrusts pierced her ankles and feet. She wept tears of pain, fear, and rage. Unable to bear the pain any longer, she turned and ran, further into the island, up the hill and in among the pale-barked birch.

The little folk stopped chasing her.

They crowded around the edge of the birch wood, jeering and

mocking, shooting their arrows but advancing no further. Ailbhe made her way to the centre of the birch wood, the highest point of the island, where the pale trunks grew thickly around her, a wooden wall that protected her from the arrows. At the crest of the hill a moss-covered standing stone leaned askew, dislodged from the earth by the roots of the trees. Ailbhe tried to read the script, but it was weathered, and the symbols seemed different from the ones she knew. She could not decipher them. She sat at the foot of the stone and peered out through the gaps between the trees. The wee folk wandered around the edge of the birch wood, calling out to her and to each other, loosing arrows that buried themselves harmlessly in the trunks of the trees.

They came no further, but neither did they leave. She was safe, for now, but she was trapped, surrounded. She knew enough of the terrible persistence of the little folk to know that they would not go away while she lived. She had to find a way to escape or starve to death where she sat.

What was it that Granny Brónach had tried to teach her about the little folk and birch woods? Ailbhe had not been paying attention. She had been too busy flirting with Flannán, too distracted by Flannán's blue eyes and red lips. If only Flannán were here now. Flannán would know what to do. But Flannán was not here. Following their apprenticeship with Granny Brónach, Ailbhe and Flannán had each been sent out, separately and alone, to find their own ways and to prove themselves in the world.

What did she know about birch trees? They were symbols of renewal and purification. Folk used brooms made from birch twigs to drive out the spirits of the old year to make way for the new. She pictured herself chasing after the wee folk waving a birch-twig broom, and she sighed. That might work–if they laughed themselves to death.

Darkness was falling. Ailbhe was exhausted, and the little folk were clearly not going to enter the birch wood. In spite of her fears, her eyes kept closing and her head nodding. She pulled out the little arrows and tended her wounds as best she could. She made a rough nest for herself among the fallen leaves and dead branches, taking care not to damage a young birch sapling that grew there, struggling up toward the light. She buried her fingers in the cold wet earth and tried to still her mind as Granny Brónach had taught her, quieting her fear, and merging her spirit with the spirits of the earth and the trees, the river, and the wind. Exhausted, she curled up and closed her eyes.

***

Ailbhe stood tall, her bark silver in the moonlight, her branches reaching into the sky, her roots deep in the earth. She felt the wind in her leaves and the worms crawling between her roots. Those roots met and intertwined with the roots of other trees, her sisters, binding the birch wood into one.

Small figures sculked around the edges of her wood and her anger smouldered. The wee folk were no threat to a full-grown tree like her, but they hated her kind, and they would gleefully cut down or root up a small sapling when they could.

She stretched out her roots, writhing through the soft, wet earth like blind, groping, vengeful fingers in search of prey.

***

A stray sunbeam woke Ailbhe, finding its way through the leafy green canopy to kiss her eyelids as she slept. She sat up and stretched, wincing and groaning, stiff and sore from her many small wounds and from sleeping awkwardly in her uncomfortable, makeshift bed. Her belly grumbled.

She needed to leave this island, or risk starving to death and spending the rest of eternity as a skeletal, undead duine gorta. She vowed to herself that if she could not escape, she would find a way to drown herself in the river. Better to drown than to be blinded, crippled, and slowly cut to pieces by the little folk.

Ailbhe picked up the heaviest, sturdiest fallen branch she could find, and hefted it as a club. If the wee folk feared the birch trees–and it seemed they did, or she would not be alive–then perhaps a birch club might be effective against them where her ash staff had failed. It was not much of a hope, but it was all she had. With the staff in her left hand and the club in her right, she crept down the hill toward the edge of the birch wood.

The little folk were nowhere to be seen. Neither was there any sound of them. Ailbhe pressed on, fearful that they had merely withdrawn a little way and were waiting in ambush. Perhaps they would leap screaming out from behind the trees, or perhaps they would drop down on her from the branches above her head? But she reached the edge of the wood and still there was no sign of them, until she saw one little green boot sticking up foot-first out of the earth.

She bent, and picked up the boot, and then she jumped back with a curse. Sticking up out of the earth was a little foot clad now only in a brown woollen sock. As she watched, the foot twitched, once, twice, and then was still. She threw the boot away and wiped her hands on a tuft of grass.

Ailbhe waded and swam across the river and climbed out on the further shore. There, the path she had been following contin-ued, winding westward between woods, hills, bogs, and lakes. By tonight she would be sure to reach a village. What a tale she would have to tell at the fire after supper. Her audience might not believe it, but that did not matter. They would enjoy the tale all the same.

At the crest of a hill, she paused, and turned to look back one last time toward the birch wood on its island in the river, its leaves burnished by the morning sun. She raised her staff in a gesture of thanks and farewell. And then she turned, and went on her way, and left the pale-barked birch trees dreaming in the sun.

The Heavenly Dreams of Mechanical Trees

Wendy Nikel

Wendy Nikel is a speculative fiction author with a degree in elementary education, a fondness for road trips, and a terrible habit of forgetting where she's left her cup of tea. Her short fiction has been published by Daily Science Fiction, Nature: Futures, and is forthcoming from Analog. Her time travel novella series, beginning with The Continuum, is available from World Weaver Press. For more info, visit wendynikel.com

originally published in *Glass & Gardens: Solarpunk Summers* from World Weaver Press

Trees were never intended to be sentient beings, or God would have created them that way, back in the Garden.

Ailanthus ponders this sometimes as the sun's rays prickle her leaves' tiny solar panels and the tubules of her stems absorb the afternoon's deluge. If the Tree of Knowledge had a voice, would it have cried out to warn the Tempted? Or would it, too, have been deceived by the Serpent and the false promises falling from its golden, forked tongue? Had it spoken, might the Tree have saved its offspring? In a way, the trees' first parents had failed them, too.

Though admittedly, Ailanthus is not a natural tree, composed of wood and leaf and bark. No, she was created by another hand, forged of copper and steel and gold, in a factory not far from the Wind Forest. Its fumes are familiar to her. As soon as they're inhaled, they're processed through her leaves and exhaled again in a form fresh and renewed. The humans planted her here, her and her brethren—miles and miles of eight-armed trees-that-aren't-trees in a forest-that-isn't-a-forest. A second Eden, created to save the world.

Whether the other trees spend their days in philosophical ponderings, Ailanthus has no way to know. Though her branches scrape theirs when the wind blows just right and their roots are irreversibly entangled, their creators gave them no means by which to communicate, so their solidarity is one of silence. Thus, Ailanthus spends her days processing the air, dreaming her dreams, and wondering what she'd say if she had the words.

Something—no, *someone* stirs at the edge of the forest, and Ailanthus shifts her attention from the skies, from the impossible flight of black-feathered birds and the way they pick the copper from her leaves' veins for their nests high in her cloud-closest branches.

***

"—with enough energy to power a hundred households for a hundred years in each and every tree."

"They're not trees." Bita's voice was hostile, accusatory. She knew how she sounded, but she didn't care. She hadn't wanted to come here anyway. The trees here cast eerie crisscrossed shadows, and the wind whistling through their branches seemed a whisper of warning.

"*Bita.*" Aunt Gigi's disapproval manifested itself in gradually deepening lines. Each wrinkle was unique: some longer, some thicker, some that oddly hooked themselves about along the contours of her face.

That, Bita thought, *is how a tree's branches ought to be.*

"Well, they're not trees," Bita said. "Not real ones, anyway. The real ones were each different. Complex and magnificent. Not like these things. These aren't even plants; they're machines—cold and hard and ugly."

"You know how long it took to build this wind forest? Decades upon decades. If it weren't for these trees and the others of their kind, Earth would be a wasteland—destroyed by years of pestilence and plague. You understand that, don't you?"

"Of course I do. I *am* a botanist."

"Botanist." Aunt Gigi snorted. "Why waste your time studying the things of the past? We need intelligent young people like you to continue the march of progress, to increase efficiency, to solve the problems of rusting roots and corroding xylem and phloem and... and these birds! Shoo! Go away! Menaces, all of them, but they're endangered species now, so what can you do? There, doesn't that sound like a problem for a scientist to solve? How to keep them from picking apart our trees without driving them into extinction as well? Or better yet, figure out how to make these trees reproduce so we don't have to replace their rusting and broken parts every decade."

Bita had stopped to study one of the trees' eight identical branches. Sure, it carried out the chemical processes of a real tree—photosynthesis, respiration, transpiration—and even produced a "green" source of energy as a byproduct, but calling these mechanical structures 'trees' was like calling a light bulb the sun.

"Please, Bita. At least consider it. We're terribly understaffed. We could use your help, and I know you could use the work."

Bita sighed and placed her hand on the nearest tree's trunk. Through the steel bark, she sensed the rushing fluids, the transference of energy pounding through the metal like a cold, mechanical heartbeat. And somehow, deep within the vibrations, somewhere among the hums and clicks and whirring of parts, Bita swore she heard a quiet voice say, "Please."

***

Ailanthus knows she's not long for this world. The harsh corrosion of her inner, movable parts produces friction and uncomfortable burns. The birds have stolen the copper from her uppermost leaves again this spring, yet not one of the trees' keepers have come around to replace them. Without these sun-nearest panels in optimal condition, she functions more slowly, barely eking out two-thirds of the energy she'd once produced each day.

The Creator once commanded the trees to reproduce: *the fruit tree yielding fruit after his kind, whose seed is in itself, upon the earth.* Perhaps His blessing is what the steel forest lacks. There was no booming, powerful "Let there be" as Ailanthus and her brethren rolled across the conveyer belt and down the assembly line, as branches were welded to trunks. There was no anointing of their roots as they were placed in the ground; no sprinkling of holy water on their leaves. Nothing but indifferent mechanical procedures and wearying nine hour shifts and the afterthought, generations later, of fruit and seed and renewal and the bitter realization that what was once deemed the world's greatest solution was really no solution at all.

***

"I told you, Steve, they want me to do the impossible. They think a botanist is some sort of wizard, some sort of Dr. Frankenstein to bring dead objects to life." As she passed by each tree, Bita placed her palm on it, just long enough to hear the rumble of its inner workings. In the months she'd been working at the wind forest, she'd done this to each tree she passed but had never experienced that small, pleading voice again. Either she'd imagined it, or she was going crazy. Mama would've said it was a sign, a message from God, but Bita hadn't believed in that sort of thing for years, since her prayers for Mama's recovery had gone unanswered.

"These forests were supposed to solve the earth's problems," she said, frowning, "but we've only created more. The factories that manufacture new trees and replacement parts are using more energy than these worn-down acres can produce. They want me to make magic, to make these trees self-replicate like the trees of the old days used to."

"What if you had a seed?" Steve asked. "An acorn, or a piece of fruit, or a pinecone? Could you do it then?"

Bita sighed. "If I had a seed? A real, viable seed? One that somehow, by some miracle, wasn't destroyed by the plague? Well, we wouldn't need these broken-down scraps of metal then, would we? It would take some time, but we could fill these rusted forests with living trees instead. Can you imagine? No more rust, no more clanking of branches when the wind blows, no more harsh glimmer of the afternoon sun reflecting off the metal panels. They say that the old trees used to have their own unique scents, that you could tell by just smelling whether you were in a forest of maple or cedar or pine. And the fruit—"

"We have fruit." Steve looked insulted, as though her words were a personal slight.

Bita laughed. "No, we don't. We have blobs of protein injected with artificial flavorings and synthetic vitamins."

"You're not going to be one of those mothers, are you?" He laughed as he took her hand.

"What do you mean?" It was Bita's turn to look insulted now.

"The kind who's obsessed with keeping her children from the evils of processed foods. Who'll spend a fortune on groceries to get real wheat and corn from halfway across the world."

"Who said I wanted to be a mother at all?"

***

Ailanthus wants nothing more than to be a mother. Nothing more than to give life. If she had the means, she would be her kind's Eve without a breeze-whisper's hesitation. *If she had the means.*

She's been listening to the young woman, watching her as she tries to solve the forest's "sustainability problem"; a problem Ailanthus equates with death. Not only her own—that she might bear bravely—but that of the forest itself.

Is there an afterlife for a forest of steel? A bright city of glory where branches won't rust, where their limbs won't snap in strong winds? And there, will they be reunited with those who've gone before? Their ancestors of fragrant wood and soft leaf?

***

"The numbers don't look good, Bita."

"Just six more months," she begged.

Not five years earlier, it was Aunt Gigi pleading for help, and now how the cogs had fully turned. Bita placed her hand on one trunk, then the next, searching for hope amid the rusting forest. Its rattling had grown so loud the women had to shout to be heard, but still Bita strained her ears, leaning in close, for some sign of that small, trusting voice.

"They're pulling our funding," Aunt Gigi said.

"Then I'll work without pay."

"We need to consider other viable options."

They both knew that there were no other *viable options*. Without the trees, the carbon dioxide levels would rise too quickly. Without the trees, everything would die.

"We need to start looking for solutions elsewhere," Aunt Gigi said.

Bita pressed her hand against another tree's trunk. "Please..."

And from somewhere deep within the clanking, clanging tree trunk, a single syllable emerged.

"Yes."

***

Ailanthus has never encountered the thing the woman calls a seed, but each day she pushes her roots out farther, searching. The seams and joints creak as they unfurl the years' worth of gnarls and reverberate as they clash against those of her brethren.

The woman presses her hand to the metal trunk and speaks of a long-ago time, when in the place where they stand there once stood a true forest with branches eternally vibrant.

"Evergreens." The whispered word echoes through Ailanthus' branches, burrows deep in her soul.

Weeks pass. The woman wearies, resting her back against the trunk as she scribbles thoughts and ideas onto a plastic tablet, then shakes her head and erases them. The sweat on her brow is slick against the trunk's steel plating, but still Ailanthus searches, calling upon her silent brethren for help.

Her roots extend, each tube stretched thin, breaking apart rock and ever searching. With the additional effort, she barely creates enough energy to keep her own processes functioning, much less power anything else. Around her, her brethren crumble and fall, carried away in beak-sized bits by the birds alighting on every branch, pecking and dismantling each leaf.

Lightning ignites the abandoned ruins, far on the forest's edge. Only the woman's swift call for help saves Ailanthus from the same fate.

Ashes to ashes, dust to dust.

***

The tree was dying. Its energy output was less than ten percent what it was just weeks ago. Still, Bita wouldn't give up. She shooed the birds from its branches and sheltered it from the rain, all while she sat in the shade of its branches and tried to devise a solution.

She soon ran out of spare parts to dull its rattling and materials to patch the rusted holes in its trunk. When a sparrow alighted upon it, it looked so natural a movement; Bita didn't even think to shoo it away until it had already tucked itself inside.

Perhaps that was what did it in, in the end.

Within moments of the bird's nesting within its trunk, the tree gave a jolt and a shudder, its branches extending one final time. The gears ground to a halt, and it let out a groan.

"Don't give up," Bita pleaded. "Look. Just look what once was."

She held up the image on her tablet of a lush, green tree in the center of a garden. *Quercus wislizeni*: the live oak.

The tree gave no sign of seeing.

***

Her limbs are immobile. Her gears are rusted stuck. Yet in that stillness comes a silence she's never experienced before. All her life has been filled with noise, the noise of mechanical parts clinking and clanking and shifting and moving. A noise she's associated with life.

But now, in the silence, she can hear those around her. Their dying thoughts fill her consciousness. The noise, the bustle, the wheels of progress which they'd so desperately tried to keep moving... that was the thing disconnecting them.

In half-whispered thoughts, Ailanthus calls upon the others. She tells them what to look for, where they might find it. And then, she waits, saving her last reserves of energy.

***

Bita fell to her knees, head bent against the metal panels so corroded that she could almost, just almost imagine that it was the roughness of true bark. Her hand dropped to the ground beside her, and there she felt... something.

There, protruding from the black soil, entwined in the mechanical tree's roots was a block of amber. Within it was something she'd only seen in pictures of long ago: the battered, half-broken, yet undeniable form of an acorn.

***

Ailanthus' branches never rust. Her leaves are always bright. She looks down upon the cloud-swirled sphere, at the bright blotches of green.

Evergreen.

Beech, Please

Maria Paige Brekke

Maria Brekke is a civil litigator living in
Minnesota with her husband, daughter,
and dog. She has taken workshops with
the Loft Literary Center and Sackett
Street Writers, and she writes short
stories in various genres. She is also
working on a young-adult fantasy novel.
Beech, Please is her first creative writing
publication.

If Rhiannon had to carve one more butterfly into a poplar's trunk, she was going to close her shop and fly away. And who would the forest's dryads turn to for body art then? Eric the Pyro Pirate, with his hackneyed hook hand and asinine wood-burning technique?

Fran hopped off the table, fluffing her leafy hair and swaying her hips to an imaginary breeze as she made her way to the mirror. She squealed in delight when she saw her reflection, twisting around to admire the image Rhiannon had spent the last two hours carving into her bark.

Rhiannon resisted the urge to roll her eyes as she started cleaning her knives. It wasn't like the butterfly was any different than the last eight she had carved. The newest trend among the poplar spirits was growing old fast.

"Willow is going to be *so* jealous," Fran gushed. "Don't tell anyone, but she went to Eric and let him burn an infinity symbol into one of her branches. From what I heard, there was a mishap with the iron, and he singed her hair. Poor thing."

"That man is a menace." Rhiannon's wings began fluttering, and she had to force her toes back onto the ground. "People have been carving pictures into trees for hundreds of years. Why go and mess with that?"

Fran nodded. "That's exactly why I came to you. I didn't want to go outside the box, end up with something weird, you know?"

"That's not what I—"

"But I guess some people like the danger of it all. Playing with fire and all that. Call me old-fashioned, but I'd rather play it safe."

Rhiannon frowned. Was her shop seen as the safe option? Stars, was she part of the *establishment* now? Rhiannon thought back to the types of clients she'd had when she opened ten years ago. Sapling dryads who were starting to spread their roots, all limbs and knots and trying to figure out what shape they wanted to be, and gnarled old crabapple spirits who were done trying to please everyone in the orchard. Lost souls and misfits. Now her customers were more often fad-chasing firs and basic birches.

Fran breezed out of Rhiannon's shop, trailing a calming scent of damp moss behind her. Rhiannon sighed. She couldn't abandon her clients to Eric's clutches, no matter how much some of them deserved his hook-handed attempts at art. Not that she had many clients these days. Fran was only her third this week.

Eric's orange neon sign flashed in the corner of Rhiannon's vision, and she glanced across the path to see her rival standing outside his studio. He was charming a group of guyads—Rhiannon's nickname for young male dryads of the bro-ish variety. They wore their vines slicked back and slouched like their arms were blanketed in snow. The guyads were all laughing at something Eric said, until a yell broke through the titters. An elm stomped up the path, pulling a young holly by her upper branches and splattering the guyads with dirt and dust.

Rhiannon stepped outside, leaning against her door. These show-downs were the best parts of her days. *What does that say about your days*, a snide voice asked, but she batted it away. A pixie had to find her fun somewhere. And this was her favorite kind of fun.

"What the fungus is this?" The elm was gesturing to a charred mark on the holly's arm, one that the holly was desperately trying to cover up.

Eric raised an infernal eyebrow. "It's an axe. Exactly what Harper asked for."

"Who do you think you are, burning something so—so *vulgar* into a young tree's bark? She's only got sixteen growth rings! And now this disgusting image is permanently on display!"

"It's her trunk, her choice," Eric said, his voice growing colder. Rhiannon caught herself nodding along, then frowned. Was she really rooting for Eric?

"Well, I never—you rotten—" the elm spluttered, then changed tactics. "It looks more like a mushroom anyway. And you call yourself an artist. Ha!"

With that, the elm swooped away. Harper slumped her shoulders and looked glumly at Eric. "It really does look like a mush-room." With that, she followed the elm, who had already set his sights on another shopkeeper to harangue.

For the first time, Eric seemed caught off guard. He rubbed his hand on the back of his neck. Then he looked across the path, and his cheeks flushed when he saw Rhiannon watching him. He kicked at the ground and went inside his shop, closing the door with a firm *click*.

And *that* was why Rhiannon couldn't throw in the towel, no

matter how empty her shop felt these days. If she closed up for good, all of the dryads in the forest would have no choice but to get their decoration from Eric, served with a hearty side of burnt leaves.

***

Rhiannon had just finished cleaning up Fran's litter—autumn in Celestia was always a letdown—when her door slammed open and Penelope lurched in. Whoever had decided to stereotype dryads as graceful had never met Penelope. She was a beech spirit who shook and reeled like a storm was battering her on even the mildest of days. She was also Rhiannon's best friend.

"Rhi Rhi," she called out. "I have the best idea for a new tattoo, and I need you to carve it now, while the inspiration is fresh."

Rhiannon and Penelope had very different aesthetics. Last month, Penelope had strong-armed her into carving "leaf and let live" into one of her branches. The time before that, it was "good things come in trees" in her roots.

"Picture this: flowing cursive, wavy lines, just about here," Penelope said, gesturing toward her collarbone area, "and it says 'beech, please.' Get it, like—"

"I get it," Rhiannon assured her friend. It was awful. And it was so very Penelope. "Come here, then. Let me do a mock-up first."

Penelope wobbled her way to the table, her roots tangling on themselves on her way there. Just as she plopped down, the door slammed open again.

"Help!" someone shouted from the doorway. "You have to help me!"

Rhiannon spun around, knife in hand. It was Gregory, one of the oak spirits. Penelope yelped and hid her face in her leaves. She was shy around the oaks.

Rhiannon rushed to the front of the store. "Are you okay? What is it?"

"Oh, it's a disaster," Gregory wailed, running his twiggy hands down his cheeks. "It was one of those awful ogres. He—oh, I can't even say it, it's just too horrible."

Gregory sank into a chair across from Penelope and lifted up his leg. On it, someone had gouged out a crude heart and attempted to carve words inside of it.

"Neil + Araminta?" Rhiannon read.

"Araminta is the mermaid he's been flirting with," Gregory said glumly. "Little heathen went and defecated my tree just to try to win her over."

"I think you mean defaced."

Gregory nodded. "That too."

"Well, he won't be winning any points for style. That's some of the worst carving I've ever seen."

It was the wrong thing to say. Gregory burst into tears. This display of emotion lent courage to Penelope, who peeked out from behind her hair. "I think it's kind of cute," she offered.

"You—you do?"

"I bet Rhiannon could just fill in the heart for you, maybe add a nice little border of vines around it, and then it'd be prettier than anything!"

Rhiannon inspected the carving more closely. "It doesn't look like he went very deep. Penelope's right, it shouldn't take too much to do a cover-up."

Gregory let out an entire breeze's worth of air in the breath he had been holding. "Oh, thank the stars. Can you do it now?"

"Sure she can," Penelope volunteered, hopping off the table. Rhiannon gave her a dark look.

But as Gregory climbed up, Rhiannon noticed something on his back. Just below his left shoulder was a series of twisted lines with a dark X in the middle. "I didn't carve that. One of Eric's?"

"What?" Gregory tried to look over his shoulder. "I don't have any tattoos."

"Yes you do," Penelope volunteered. "A yummy one right here." She poked the X on his back.

Rhiannon inspected it more closely. The lines looked like they were guiding the eye to the X, almost like— "Gregory. Why do you have a treasure map on your back?"

The door slammed open for a third time. "Did someone say treasure map?" Standing in the doorway, with his hip cocked, his eye patch arranged jauntily over his face, and his hook raised proudly in the air, was Rhiannon's nemesis. Arch-nemesis, even. Eric the pirate-turned-wood-burner.

"Am I being punished for something?" Rhiannon grumbled to herself.

But five minutes later, Rhiannon was bent over Gregory's back, staring at the meaningless squiggly lines until her eyes began to water, trying to ignore Eric's infuriating humming.

Finally, Eric couldn't keep it in any longer. "It's obvious, isn't it? Or is this a map only a pirate can read?" When no one answered, he stroked his beard with his hook. His smile grew even more smug. A few minutes ago, Rhiannon would have bet her shop that no one could have looked more like an asshole than Eric did standing in that doorway, but leave it to him to beat his own record for assholery.

"The only thing that's obvious to me is that this is the work of an amateur. For all I know, the ogre got bored and started doodling on Gregory's back."

Eric gaped. "What? No! This is leagues better than 'Neil + Araminta.' Definitely someone with a real knack for wood art."

"Will you please stop rambling and tell us what you know?"

"I will, my dear Rhiannon." He paused dramatically. "For a price."

"If you mean the treasure, I've decided we should split it equivocally," Gregory said, twisting to look at them.

"He means equitably," Rhiannon supplied.

"I don't want money," Eric said, swatting the air with his hook. "I want in. I want to be part of your shop. Can't you see it? The pirate burner and the pixie carver working together to beautify the forest one tree at a time?"

"No. Absolutely not."

Eric looked at Penelope and Gregory. "We go together like moss on a tree, don't we?"

Penelope nodded, her twigs bouncing. The traitor.

"If you mean that you will always be in my shadow, then you're right," Rhiannon snapped.

Eric shrugged. "If you want me to help you find the treasure, those are my terms."

He was the most infuriating pirate that had ever lived. But Rhiannon thought about her empty appointment book and her depleting savings account. The memory of those guyads crowding around Eric was still fresh. Maybe with him around, she would be able to draw clients back in.

"Fine. If you get us the treasure, I'll let you come work in my shop."

"*When* I lead you to the treasure, I will gladly work side-by-side in *our* shop."

Rhiannon sighed. "Just tell me where we need to go."

***

Rhiannon slammed her empty margarita glass onto the bar at the lagoon tavern. She glanced over to where Penelope and Gregory were dancing, twisting their branches up into the air like saplings, having given up all pretenses of looking for gold. "I don't see any treasure here."

The mermaid who swam up to take Rhiannon's glass huffed. "You're no prize either, hon."

"We aren't here for the treasure. We're here for the next clue," Eric explained.

"Well? Where is it?"

Before Eric could answer, the tavern exploded in a cacophony of shrieking and chatter. A birchelorette party descended on the bar, filling the place with drunken giggles and a confetti of winged seeds.

"I told you to stop planting yourselves in here," one of the mermaids shouted from the lagoon behind the bar, but none of the birchelorettes listened.

Rhiannon was sweeping seeds out of her hair when one of the dryads noticed her. "Ohh, you're the carver, aren't you? Girls, it would be so much fun to get carvings together, don't you think?"

The shrieking somehow got even louder.

"Could you do me? I love the patterns on your wings. Would you carve me a butterfly to match?" a second dryad said, draping her arm-branch across the bar.

If Rhiannon never saw another butterfly, it would be too soon. Honestly, she was going to have to try really hard not to take out her frustration on real butterflies from now on. She had no such reservations with the insipid birch spirit invading her space. "Go fall in a forest and see if anyone hears you."

Unfortunately, everyone heard *that*. The chatter finally quieted, so much that Rhiannon could hear the last few seeds plopping to the ground.

The dryad glared daggers at Rhiannon and tossed her leafy hair back. "Girls, let's go. Some people just don't know how to have a good time."

Eric gave Rhiannon a sidelong look after the birchelorettes left. "That's your problem, you know. That attitude is why you're losing clients to me."

"Excuse me?"

"We both know you're a better artist than me. Stars, the whole forest knows. But sometimes people just want to feel special. They want their ideas to be appreciated, or at least not be made to feel like an idiot for wanting something pretty or trendy."

Rhiannon felt something uncomfortably close to shame twist in her chest, but she pushed it down. "You planning to become a therapist next? I wouldn't bother, you're as bad at it as you are at body art."

She meant to tease him, throw a jab to defend herself from his gaze, but the words swung out of her like a sword.

Eric flinched. "You know what? You like to think you're all tough or whatever, but you're really just mean. Maybe you deserve to go out of business." He stood up and flipped the bar stool he had been sitting on upside down. The bottom of the seat was scratched to hell. "Here's your damn clue."

Rhiannon sat for a minute, stunned. But Gregory and Penelope materialized behind her, twittering about the clue.

Some say our bark is worse than our bite,
But our spite might the whole forest ignite
Knock thrice if you wish to join us,
but you'd better be deciduous.

Stars above.

Penelope tilted her head. "Is it a riddle?"

"Worse. It's the Bough No More club pledge," Rhiannon said, shuddering as she remembered stumbling over the choppy meter at club meetings. Her mother had been furious when Rhiannon joined the group of malcontents, especially when she chopped off her hair and dyed her incandescent purple wings a deep black to match it. Rhiannon hadn't lasted long in the club, and the black dye faded soon after, but she kept the pixie cut as she began carving a name for herself.

Gregory gulped. "You don't think we have to go there, do you? From what I've heard, the Bough No Mores can be quite," he dropped to a whisper, "voluptuous."

Rhiannon cocked her head.

"Volatile, I think," Eric murmured. He seemed recovered, but he didn't quite meet Rhiannon's eyes.

Gregory nodded solemnly.

"Grow your sense of adventure!" Eric clapped Gregory on the back, forcing an extra pinch of swashbuckling into his words. "Danger is part of the hunt, and we must meet it with aplomb!"

"We're real treasure hunters now!" Penelope squealed, clapping her hands so hard she fell off her stool.

***

Rhiannon still remembered the pattern for the three knocks on the makeshift door to the Bough No More Club's cave. After she knocked, there was some loud whispering, then the door creaked open. Harper, the holly from Eric's shop, stood on the other side, a scrap of cloth tied around her arm.

"Who is it, babe?" a voice called from inside.

"Um ... it's that woodburner pirate guy and a bunch of old people."

"I'm thirty-four, you—"

Eric put his hand on Rhiannon's arm and cut her off. Again.

"We're hoping to find something here. Some kind of clue. Would you mind if we took a look around?"

Harper shrugged and opened the door the rest of the way. "Do whatever you want. Not like I own the place."

Harper walked back to the table, where a magnolia spirit was bent over some papers. No one else was in the cave, which had seen a makeover since Rhiannon had last attended a meeting. *More than a decade ago,* said an unwelcome voice in her head. The club had put up string lights and strewn bright rugs across the stone floor. Overstuffed sofas sat in place of the austere wooden chairs. The only thing Rhiannon recognized was the phrase written on the back wall of the cave in an artistic scrawl: *Bough No More.* It had been her one meaningful contribution to the club.

"Where is everyone?" Rhiannon asked Harper.

"I dunno, probably at work?"

The original Bough No Mores would be ashamed.

"What exactly are we looking for?" Penelope asked.

"A clue can take many forms," Eric said sagely. "Look for anything out of place or unusual."

Rhiannon was meandering around a circle of bean-bag chairs when Harper crumpled the papers on the table and threw them away from her with an "Augh!" The wad landed at Rhiannon's feet.

The magnolia put her arm around Harper and shot Eric a dirty look. "It's okay, we just have to keep practicing. We'll get it right eventually."

Rhiannon picked up the papers and unrolled them. They were

all drawings of mushrooms. No, not mushrooms. Axes. "Are you trying to fix your tattoo?"

Across the room, Eric let out an undignified squeak and dropped whatever he was holding.

The magnolia eyed Rhiannon. "How do you know about that?"

"That elm was shouting about it loud enough for the whole forest to hear."

Harper put her head in her hands and muttered something about "dads" and "so embarrassing."

"Come on, it can't be that bad. Show me what we're working with." Rhiannon nodded to Harper's arm. Eric was hovering at the edge of the table, shuffling awkwardly.

Harper unwrapped the fabric and revealed the tattoo. Rhiannon schooled her face into a blank expression. It was worse than she thought. She glanced at Eric, and his ears turned bright red.

"See?" Harper groaned. "It's mortifying."

Rhiannon's hand itched. She grabbed a pencil and paper. "It's fixable. You need more depth in the handle and some shading to bring out the steeliness of the axe. Sharper lines too."

She showed them the sketch. They were silent for a minute, and then Harper started to cry.

"What did I do?" Rhiannon mouthed to Eric.

Rhiannon was enveloped in a leafy hug. "Can you really make it look like that?" Harper sniffled.

"Of course," Rhiannon said, looking bemusedly over Harper's foliage at Eric. But Eric was studying the drawing, his head cocked as he followed the lines of the axe like it was another treasure map.

"I don't have my tools with me now," Rhiannon said as Harper let go of her. "But come by my shop tomorrow and we'll fix it right up."

Harper retreated back to the magnolia, who planted a gentle kiss on her lips. "I told you we'd figure it out."

Harper nodded, looking gratefully at Rhiannon. Then, she gestured to the door. "Your clue's on the doorframe. I noticed it this morning."

Rhiannon moved toward the door, but Eric stopped her. "Rhiannon, I—" he took a deep breath. "I was wondering if you could teach me to draw like you do. Everything you make is so beautiful, and my stuff just never turns out how I want it to. I keep practicing, but I'm not sure I'm even getting better."

Huh. Rhiannon paused as she thought about how to answer. "You've got an eye for it," she said. "You just need to pay more attention to perspective, and that will solve a lot of your problems. I'd be happy to show you some things, if that's what you want." She hoped he could sense the apology in her words.

Eric beamed at her like she had just presented him with a chest full of glistening treasure, and her breath caught in her throat.

"The clue's here!" Penelope shouted from the doorway. Rhiannon, grateful for the escape, rushed over.

"*The true treasure lies within?*" Gregory asked. "What's that supposed to mean?"

"I have no idea," Rhiannon said, her heart sinking. "But it doesn't look like a clue to me."

"Ooh, Gregory, don't you see? Whoever drew that map on you wanted you to look inside yourself and see your own worth!" Penelope did a happy dance, knocking over a fern with her hip. "You have a fairy godmother somewhere!"

Rhiannon's eyes caught on the words she had carved on Penelope's hip months ago. She had cringed as she etched the phrase onto her friend's body, but now...*good things come in trees.* "Gregory. The treasure is inside you."

"I get it," he said. "I need to recognize the value that I bring, no matter how empty I sometimes feel."

"No," Rhiannon said. "It's not a bullshit moral, it's another clue. Gregory, the treasure is *inside* you. Or more accurately, inside your tree."

Gregory's mouth dropped open. "Inside my—oh, come on! Of all the invasive species, pirates have got to be the worst."

"Or the best, depending on how you look at it," Eric said, flashing his pearly whites. "Got any hollows we can dig around in?"

"You wood-n't dare."

Rhiannon put a reassuring hand on Gregory's shoulder. "Just take us to your tree and I'll remove all of your unwanted body art, free of charge."

Gregory thought for a minute. "I have one stipulation. You throw in a carving too. I've always thought it would be cool to have a bird on my shoulder, here-ish."

Rhiannon almost groaned. But then she caught Eric's knowing, twinkling, singular eye. She released her clenched teeth and attempted a smile. "I'd be delighted."

"I love that idea," Penelope gushed. "Maybe I can get a matching one."

Gregory's leaves reddened as he blushed.

But he took them to his tree. And there, in a hollow at its base, sat a gleaming pile of gold coins.

If Gregory's leaves had been tinged red before, they glowed like a sunset when Penelope grabbed the gold from his hollow with a triumphant squeak.

She presented it to Rhiannon, dropping at least a dozen pieces of gold in the process. "Two matching birds, please."

Rhiannon grinned at her friend. "A deal's a deal."

***

Rhiannon stood outside her shop, staring up at the new sign. *Cutting Flame*, with accents of fire and shadow. The pirate beside her flashed a self-satisfied grin.

"I know you hid that treasure," she told him out of the corner of her mouth. "No one else would have burned an X into that map."

"Even if I *did* know what you were talking about, any treasure-hiding was clearly conducted to help Gregory learn about self-confidence and for no other purpose."

"Of course it was. And like I said before, a deal's a deal. But Eric?"

"Yes?"

"You're doing all of the butterflies from now on. Every. Damn. One."

The Trimming of the Branches

Ali Miller

My father's life belonged to the orchard. So, too, in her day, had his mother's life belonged to the orchard, and his mother's mother, and his mother's mother's father, and so on. My grandmother loved it like a curse, grinding her sweat and her body into the dirt until her arms were thin like saplings. She died in its arms, asleep in a chair carved out of the bones of a mulberry tree as old as she was, and then the orchard was my father's, as it would one day be mine.

In this way, the orchard was my entire world, though it was not my life. All I ever knew in my life was trees; trees, and my father tall and proud guiding them with gentle hands, determined to be kinder than my grandmother ever was. This was my childhood, raised as much by the trees as by my father, who kept a distracted eye on the trees at all times. As he told it, I was half-daughter, half-tree, plucked from a limb when I was ripe enough to be born, sprouted from the dirt an unexpected gift. Perhaps there was some truth in his story, for I did run wild and free through the orchard. My knees plowed the soil while I learned to crawl. My nimble little hands plucked pears and peaches and cherries and countless other fruits as soon as I was strong enough to climb. The trees were my kin, in this way, and more familiar to me than my father, who often spent nights half buried in the soil beneath the trees.

There was a time, before I knew any better, that I was jealous of the trees. How can you be jealous of a thing that you love? And yet it gnawed at me like a woodpecker, the envy, the longing, the empty space where his attention might belong. I dogged his heels for weeks, waiting for him to notice me, dragging my feet in the soil and disrupting the planting season. I planted blackberries out by the fig trees, but he only fought the brambles back. He never lost his temper. He would wait patiently for me to be out of the way and then fit his big hand over the crown of my head, squeeze a little as if he could impart some of his placid calm on me, and then set to fixing things.

One night I snuck out of bed and found him sleeping out beneath the moon, crying in his sleep. His tears were watering the trees. After that, somehow, I found I could not muster up my same old jealousy. Wouldn't any creature have preferred his gentle touch over his weeping?

He had always seemed sturdy. It was staggering to learn that he could cry. In all the ways that my grandmother had been stooped and cracking open, he was smooth and steadfast, the kind of person you could trust to hold you. In his lifetime he had mastered the art of cutting short the limbs of the trees, cutting off the dead leaves for the tree's own good. Keeping them healthy. Even as he grew old, he stood up straight and tall and performed this task without flinching. He cupped my head with his palm, still. He took care of things.

When my father knew that it was his time, he dug himself a grave in the very center of the orchard. He dug it deep and true, measured with his precise eye, under the waning light of the day. The trees rustled around him, singing him a mourning song, which he acknowledged with a nod. When the grave was dug, he set the shovel aside, lay down inside the hole, and swept the dirt back over himself in a neat little pile, and I think that somewhere in the ground he must have started crying.

The next day when I opened my eyes there was a knowledge at the heart of me that I must till the ground by the lemon trees, so powerful an urge that it surely was the thing that woke me. I went out to look at the orchard which I supposed was my life now. My father's touch lingered in ways that I had never noticed before, such as the shape of the branches of the apple trees and the defeated slump of the ambitious blackberry brambles. With my new knowing eyes, I could see the orchard through to the ground and the roots. This was how my father had seen the orchard.

In the fresh new dirt at the very center of the orchard stood a tree, big and sturdy and towering, and on the tree grew a fruit I had never seen before, more luscious and true in color than any other. I walked on. All around me, the orchard was blooming. The little nubs of the branches my father had trimmed were healing over. The trees were still growing.

And this is the story of your birth: one day, a tree grew you.

Unlike my father, and my father's mother, and my father's mother's mother, my life belongs to you. I am raising you in spite of the orchard, my daughter. My eyes are on you, sweet thing.

When you are ready, I will teach you to plant your feet and grow roots and open your face up to the sun and the rain. I will hold you close when we sleep. I will teach you to climb trees and we will let the orchard grow a little wild, like me. I can feel it starting to get ambitions, thinking itself a forest. Is that what it will be for you? Is that what you are going to teach it to be?

Those blackberry brambles have crept ever inwards, but the fig trees are learning to hold their own. A river is growing in the empty footprints that my father left behind. Every morning, I wake up to the sound of what the trees are saying, with a pressure in my head that is shaped like an orchard. But you need me too. The trees are learning self-sufficiency.

I understand, now, the things my father could not tell me. I am watering you with his love for me. I am trying to do better. I am pruning the father-tree.

End of the World, Beginning of Everything

Kiersten Gonzalez

Kiersten is a fiction-lover, especially when a story has more than meets the eye. She holds a Master's in Writing from Seton Hall University and works as a medical copywriter. Of all the small joys in life, she'd rate a slice of chocolate cake ***1. You can find her musings on books and writing via Instagram: @ kiersten.writes

That's where I'm going, my husband said as he forcefully shut the suitcase, the last of his belongings haphazardly thrown in it. He told me he was leaving for Ushuaia, the lowest part of South America.

Significa 'fin del mundo, principio de todo.'

¡Ah, mirá vos! I remarked. How about that—a place called "end of the world, beginning of everything."

He marched toward the doorway and paused, framed in the narrow wood trim. Quietly, like an afterthought, he asked, "Do you want to come with me?"

Flashes of our life ran through my mind like a film reel, my heart producing just enough light to brighten the images. I refocused on his eyes, brows drawn in frustration, hand squeezing the door frame as if he would rip it from the hinges.

No. Volá, I said. In other words: *get out of here.*

So he left, and faded to a phantom. I stayed in Buenos Aires for one month. Then I decided to come to America. To a place I could pronounce easily, because it was like Spanish: *California.* I would become an actress, the dream that gave my husband that faraway, unbelieving look in his eyes. Maybe there would be a beginning for me too.

***

The journey started so easily. No flight delays. Not even turbulence. I gathered all of my luggage without difficulty in the Colorado airport. I planned first to stay with my friend from university, to get comfortable in America before going on my own. I had made Argentina feel like her home when she studied abroad. She was happy to do this also, for me.

Colorado. Spanish for *red-colored.* Red, like my face blushing as I asked a third time for the internet connection password at the airport front desk. Hours had passed without my friend coming to retrieve me. My new life was so fragile that it depended on the correct spelling of the connection code, and the steady glow of three arched bars.

When I reached her, she explained that her sister-in-law had passed suddenly. Hit by a drunk driver. My friend had to fly to her brother, to help with his two small children. She hoped I understood.

I scribbled her address on my arm. She told me to drive her car and stay in the apartment like it was my home. She would be back, eventually, to help me too.

My voice shook uncontrollably as I sat in the taxi and recited the address to the driver. He asked me repeatedly why I was crying. I pretended I did not understand him.

In the apartment, I spent much time scanning the newspapers and magazines about the town. The articles detailed events and restaurants, with photos of happy families. There was one note in the newspaper, an entry under JOB POSTINGS that caught my eye.

ACTORS/PERFORMERS: *Does the thought of haunting excite, rather than scare you? Do you understand the emotions of faraway souls, whose presence lingers? Ghost tour guides needed. Inquire at the Visitor's Center.*

***

The worker on the phone had not specified what to wear to the interview. I wore my regular clothes. Jeans, a sweater. I put on a wool coat. Argentina is not sunny all year, but this mountain air does not suit me. I go to bed with socks like furry creatures on my feet, a clinging knit cap, and still, I wake up cold.

When I explained who I was to the worker at the visitor's center, I thought the man was laughing at my English, which needed improvement, but he said, "How do you expect to lead ghost tours dressed like that?" I apologized many times; I did not know how I should present myself for the interview. The man, Mr. Thistle, handed me a folder and told me to come back tomorrow. He added, "Sorry, darling."

I sheepishly took the folder. That night I took out its contents, particularly the photos of the other tour guides. They were dressed like my great-grandparents. Vests with little buttons, tall hats, and puffy blouses. I sat for a long time at the small kitchen table, tucked into the corner of the apartment, and wondered how I might become like these people.

***

The next day I marched through melting piles of snow, down the main street of the historic ski town, back to the visitor's center. Groups of families and their acquaintances stood aside. They wore large sunglasses like bug eyes, silk scarves around their heads and draping from their pockets. Even their shoelaces looked expensive; they stood up straight, and did not droop as laces should from excessive wear.

They snickered as I strode past in a black lace tango dress that had belonged to my mother. I had thought it would be helpful for auditions in Los Angeles. I found a black turtleneck to go underneath the plunging neckline and wool tights to cover my legs. The ruffles of fabric flowed with each step, revealing my friend's brown snow boots and hiding them in the next stride, like a curtain opening and closing. A headband fashioned from a piece of dark lace covered the side of my face. In my apartment, I stared doubtfully at the outfit laid on the bed. But I straightened my back now, because these people would never be as brave as me.

On the second floor of the imitation log cabin, Mr. Thistle was organizing books behind a desk. When he turned, his eyes brightened.

"Hey, honey! Thanks for coming back." He sounded very much how I imagined an American cowboy to talk.

"Hello, thank you very much."

"I love your accent—Romanian? Sounds like Transylvania. Feels spooky."

"I am from Argentina." I emphasize the harder g that we would roll over smoothly in Spanish.

"You reviewed the folder?"

I nod.

"Great. You gotta know these stories inside and out, like you're really a ghost."

"I understand."

"The outfit is perfect. Different. Has a *latino* flair, you know?"

I was not sure of his meaning but I nodded. It was not as good as a movie role, or even a minor role on television. But the advertisement said "acting." How could I work at a restaurant, or the grocery store, knowing I passed the chance to be an actress in this town?

He asked more questions, logistical-type concerns, and after that, I signed the paperwork to make it official.

I successfully became a ghost.

***

"Oh, hello! I did not see you all there."

I hold a big black binder with my notes but only take fast glances at its contents. I talk loudly, because Americans seem to speak at high volumes. When I speak louder, I tremble less. An oversized lantern swings in my hand, meant to light our way in an aesthetic manner. It has a real candle inside that drips wax in pools of milky puddles. Though beautiful, I must spend hours scraping it clean, until my knuckles splinter and bleed.

"Yes, I lived here a long time ago. And I have seen many *soopertitious* things. Come, and I will tell you my stories."

As I tell the stories, the names meld together. They all sound the same to me. A young couple whispers to each other, then slowly walks away from the group, as if I will not notice. But I do notice, and I hear their whispers about me. My accent, my strange clothes.

***

There was a rumor floating around the town that the innkeeper's wife, Maria, had gone back to her old ways and become a companion to the mining men. Though it was not true, and she loved him very much, the inn owner came home in a rage. She was so frightened that she had a heart attack, and died hours later. Since then, the inn has been sold many times. They say Maria haunts the halls, scaring away customers from her home.

A few years ago, a woman staying at the inn went to shower in the bathroom on the top floor, since another was occupied. The bathroom did not seem recently cleaned or used, but the light came on when she flipped the switch. As she showered, she heard the door slam from the other side of the curtain. She called out, but only silence answered. The water started running very hot and burned her skin. The woman could not turn off the water and so she hurried out of the shower. As she dried off, the mirror shattered. The woman ran out of the hotel in her towel, blood dripping from her legs and feet. When they investigated, they found the water pipes had been taken out of the bathroom many years ago. The owner left the inn shortly after.

Though many faces on the tour show raised eyebrows and slight frowns as I finish the story, there is one young girl with bright eyes of wonder.

"Why does she act that way?"

The answer seems obvious. Perhaps she missed part of the story. "She is very angry, because she did not think she deserved that treatment."

"But the husband thought she didn't love him anymore. Couldn't she forgive him?"

Feet pace back and forth in the small crowd surrounding me. I do not have a good answer.

"Maybe if I see her, I will ask her."

While packing up my binder and papers into my bag they fall and spread across the front porch of the inn. When I raise my head from picking them up, a woman's face stares back at me in the window. Blood rushes under my cheekbones, constricting my insides and stealing my breath.

The face is mine though. A reflection.

Maybe the wife did not know how.

***

On one evening, I must redirect the tour in a different direction from my usual route, because there is another guide who has gone the wrong way. The situation is minor but she does not even look sorry for interrupting me. I act nicely and my flock of backpacks and relentless picture-taking follows.

The road slants upward; we climb to the neighborhood where more affluent citizens lived, where they could survey the people below. I look in my binder discreetly to practice the characters' names and that is why the blooming tree, enormous, with curving black branches, surprises me.

Large boughs of flowers in varying shades of vivid purple bounce in the breeze. So similar to the trees that bloom in Buenos Aires, though it is winter here, not the springtime of South America. There are no other colorful plants on the street, which is dark except for the occasional shimmer of snow in a headlight. As we walk to an old haunted inn, I see there is someone tending it, before the tree disappears from view.

The next day is my day off, the one weekday that I do not lead tours. Even so, I have gone into town, dressed in my own clothes instead of a costume. The morning is bright. Skiers in puffy coats and goggles walk along the sidewalk, looking for a meal or a trinket in the shops. I visit a café to purchase a tea, something earthy and strong, and with the paper cup warming my hands, I start up the road.

Retracing my steps, I estimate where the tree should be. There is only a small, empty field between a house and an abandoned restaurant. I cannot tell if it is a park or simply a clearing, but there is no tree. I stand for a while, flipping my silver wedding ring around my fingers. I make my way back home confused, with an emptiness in my chest and a lingering tingle in my hands and toes.

***

About the time when I start to settle in my borrowed home, a letter arrives from my mother.

She says she misses me. The city is not the same without me. She slid a few dried flowers between the rustling paper sheets, because, "with a text message you cannot capture, cannot hold home." There is a pain, a lump in my throat, as I trace the delicate, flat veins.

At the close of the letter, my mother writes, "Roberto called to check in...he's been thinking of you." My jaw tenses. Beto should not have had any concern for them. She copied an address and a phone number at the bottom of the paper.

I fold the paper back into its envelope and slide it into a stack of books on the table, so that it is mostly hidden, but still easy to find.

***

The visitors place large bills in my jar as they leave and I pack the tips carefully away. As I walk down the street, a purple glow radiates in the distance. My heart pulses wildly.

The trunk is thick and sheltering, with knotted branches that twist and curve. It's as if it has a heartbeat, a hum beneath the bark. A yellow spotlight on the corner of the abandoned restaurant coats the tree and the clearing in a haunting glow.

There is a rustle from behind a low-hanging branch. A young man turns around from the other side of the trunk.

"I'm sorry, I did not see you—I did not mean to disturb you," I say.

"Please, don't be sorry." The dusk sky, lit from the sun dipping below the horizon, illuminates his deep blue eyes, which seem to reflect the stars.

"I'm happy you saw it."

"I had come in the daytime and could not find it, but now, when it is becoming dark, I found it quite easily."

"Yes, it's funny how things like that can happen. Disappear, and sometimes reappear." He chuckles quietly. We exchange names. His name is Marcel.

"Do you often come to this tree?" I ask.

He nods apprehensively. "I've become a bit like its caretaker."

I lift a group of flowers. The fragrance is overwhelmingly of vanilla.

"Your dress is very interesting," he says. "It's like a tango dress."

"Ah. I do not normally dress like this. It is for work." I tell him how I direct ghost tours.

"You must be very confident."

"I was not at first. My groups did not go well. People did not like that I seemed strange to them. But it is getting better." I stop short and hurriedly gather my belongings. "I should be going now, before it is very late."

"I understand," he says. "Will I see you here again?" There is a hint of a plea in his voice.

"If I can find it, yes, I hope so."

"I think you'll be able to."

***

I duck under the canopy of flowers and into the sweet-smelling space and sit on a nearby branch. Marcel leans against the trunk next to me.

"You found it again," he says. He sounds genuinely surprised.

"You seem to think I would not be able to find it. It's very large. And bright."

"That's true." His mouth twitches as if deciding on words, but he stays quiet.

"This tree reminds me so much of home," I say.

"Yes. It makes a space feel familiar. Safe."

I do not think the feeling is only produced by the tree. There is something familiar about Marcel, too.

In the darkness, the light from the corner of the abandoned restaurant illuminates the snow falling silently. I look up to the branches, to the clusters of flowers, and expect to see them covered in icy flakes, but they are bare and bright. The snow dissolves into their glowing color.

I rehearse the questions in my mind, searching for words. *How are they resistant to the cold?* It seems Marcel is challenging me—seeing if I will inquire after the thoughts he protects.

I start to ask but pause at the sound of voices approaching from the sidewalk. Through the flowers and leaves, a couple draws close from the main street. I scoot closer behind the trunk, anticipating that they will also want to explore the blossoming branches. But with faces turned to the ground, they slosh past.

I whisper to Marcel, "How could they do that?"

"They didn't see it," Marcel says.

"But this tree is huge. I have not seen another bloom like it here."

"If they'd seen it, I'm sure they would stop."

"If? Only some people can see it?"

He hesitates, but answers. "Yes."

"So it is not real?" I push against a branch but it bounces with my shifting weight.

"It *is* real. Not everyone can see it."

Had it not been that the tree was so beautiful—if it wasn't that the warmth of Marcel reminded me of the dusty, fire smell of charcoal in the city, and his sweetness the smell of dulce de leche—I would have run far away from the place in a panic. But I did not run. Like anyone, I was drawn to what reminded me of home.

"Have you felt a desire so strong, you're sure it will make you happy?"

I nod wordlessly.

"Close your eyes."

Wind threads through the branches above us, creating a comforting whoosh and causing a cascade of soft speckles to tumble over us. I like the coolness on my skin, relieving for a moment the heat of panic and desire competing in my blood.

My legs sway when I open my eyes. We are on top of a hill, facing a valley of lights—a city, blinking like a creature awake and breathing. There is no chill, no cloud of vapor when I breathe. Instead pillowy warmth tickles my cheeks and I remove my coat. Marcel stands next to me, in the same spot he had been in, hands on his waist as he looks out into the crater of lights.

"Where are we?" I ask.

"Not sure. I think Los Angeles."

Los Angeles?

"This is imaginary though—a vision? A dream?" I ask.

He bends down, scoops a handful of sand and throws it toward my dress. The dirt glistens like glitter on the hem. "It's all real. It always is. What did you think of?"

Staring at Marcel, my eyes dry in the desert air. "I thought of becoming an actress. In Hollywood. That's why I came to America."

"So that is how it works..." Marcel traces his fingers across the trunk.

"What do you mean?"

He raises his head with a look of sadness. A fist forms and releases repeatedly in his hands.

"I first saw the tree wandering through the streets at night. My girlfriend told me she was leaving. It ended my world. I couldn't just watch her pack. So I walked out, passing time until I thought she had definitely driven away. I was so empty—the beauty filled me. I felt safe, like being at my grandma's house. I shut my eyes thinking of her. She died years ago. When I opened my eyes, I was on the front lawn of her old house. The mail carrier was sticking a few envelopes in the mailbox. He asked if I was okay. I said I wasn't sure, then gestured at the tree. He didn't see anything."

This is the familiarity I recognized in Marcel: the seeking, the longing.

"So it is like a spirit?"

"A ghost tree? I guess so. Have you ever heard of such a thing? It appears and disappears, and draws close to those who are missing something."

His look is guarding accusation, tip toeing around the question that hangs heavy.

"You must be wondering how I could see it, too."

He nods. I tell him of everything I had lost in Argentina.

Marcel says, "I imagined my whole life with her: kids, warm dinners, cool evenings— everything. I saw it so clearly, as if that vision would make it real. Suddenly, with the tree, that's possible." He sighs. "Sometimes you just want to escape. As if you can become someone else."

"I understand." My shoulders sink.

We stay for a while, watching over the city. Was the tree strange? Was all of it strange? Of course. But Marcel understood why it was so easy to accept: we also felt strange, and separated from the world.

***

"Why don't we go together, and never come back."

Marcel and I walk through a hedge maze in the English countryside. Our tree stands just outside of it, gleaming in the moonlight to our eyes only.

"Go where?"

"Anywhere—anywhere in the world. Wherever you want."

"We already do. We have gone to many places."

"I mean forever. As far as I know, you and I are the only people who can see the tree. That means something, doesn't it?"

Doesn't it? It must mean something. A light of hope that had been shut within me flickered hesitantly, flirting with the idea of shining.

"Wherever I want?"

Marcel smiles. "Yes."

In the distance, a window brightens in the historic estate. A single naked bulb in the shadowy, towering structure with spires. A ghost? Perhaps.

I tell Marcel, "I have to think."

***

The mail comes late in the day so I always receive it in the dark, once I have returned from work. Tonight's small stack from the metal mailbox contains something heavy and different among the store circulars and coupons.

My stomach churns as I turn on the light and see the handwriting. The stamp on the envelope shows two tango dancers locked in an embrace. It looks ridiculous, such an exaggerated symbol of my country, but I look down at my work attire and how I appear as an identical symbol.

Beto's neat, graceful penmanship spans many pages. From where did all these words come, from the man who for months had nothing to say?

The trip here was very long, my neck was cramped for days...I find the grocery stores do not stock the same items, it is inconvenient... I am getting acclimated to the lack of sun, mostly clouds...There was a sea lion lying on a rock...

These are empty details. How is it that he is still giving me the run around, when I am nearly at the top of the world and he is at its bottom? I am about to throw away the thick stack of paper until I fold it, and see the last page.

I don't know how to say this—I have written these details thinking their meaning might become apparent. I should not send this to you. But these details—they are my life, without you.

I reread the rest of the letter, taking my time with the details. *I was so foolish...no words seemed right...* There are reflective sentences, moments of clarity threaded throughout.

I felt if I escaped, it would fix me. I think, now, that it was a lie.

***

Leaving forever with Marcel meant leaving behind acting, the small job that I had become fond of, and the little independence I had built. But part of me was only floating through and, at times, unable to make contact.

The place I chose to go had to be better than my dream and I could not think of one. Instead, I imagined a location based on its features. A slightly broken place that could be made exquisite if only it had a little love and a lot of hard work. A longing burns in my chest, and shakes in my bones. I trust the tree will understand my deepest desires.

I stuff my belongings back into the suitcases I had so hopefully carried to America weeks ago. As I walk through the town, I see a tour group in the distance. I would miss the ghosts and those lovely people. I forget them when I see Marcel waiting for me, his smile warm, his eyes assuring.

"Are you ready?" he asks. He holds a leather trunk in each hand.

"Yes."

The air becomes wet. Not in droplets, but invisibly damp around us. We've been brought near the coast, the churning of water hushing the slow hum of life in this place. Behind us, tall mountains rise from a scene of bold colors, their white snowy tips branching into streaks. If it was not for the climate, I would have thought we were still in Colorado.

"Where are we?" Marcel asks. We stand under the tree, in the middle of a quiet park.

"I am not sure."

I had imagined the path would be clear. I thought the tree would lead us to a little shelter, something empty but comforting. A place that seemed right for two lost people.

Then I see it. Across the street, the house is sunny yellow with white trim. Plush grass surrounds it, vines with red flowers creep and twist up a wood fence with bumps and knots. Two rocking chairs sway on the front porch. The chairs are not near each other. One is in the corner. The other is closer to the stairs, with empty bottles underneath it. A cigar sits on the windowsill near it, ashy smoke rising from its end.

Through the wide bay window, I see Beto sitting at a small table, dipping a pastry into a ceramic cup. Steam floats from the liquid and wraps around his face. He dips the pastry three times and I exhale. Stillness. There is nothing to worry about in this place, except how much honey is still left in the jar, and when the sun will set. And yet, what are his glazy eyes imagining, and what sounds play in his head?

"Where are we?" Marcel asks again, voice shaking a little this time.

Beto turns his gaze toward us and I wrap behind the other side of the trunk. Does he see the tree too? Or only the back of a strangely familiar woman?

"That man," I start.

Marcel looks across the street, shoulders leaning forward. When he turns to me again his mouth twitches as it always did when he was looking for words. His face settles into the expression I feel on my face. Slight frown, eyes quivering with emotion but lids settled heavily on top. It is surprise, confusion, and disappointment.

"He is your..."

I nod.

The stolenness of his heavy sigh is familiar. At one time it was my own.

***

I avoid the tree for many days after our return. But without any ghost tours to lead, without anything at all to do, I think of it constantly.

On an evening when I am feeling brave, I go back to town. I had unfinished business with the tree, which acted in clever riddles to me.

Even from only a block away, it's obvious that the clearing is bare. There is no tree. Despite the absence, the air lingers strongly with vanilla. A few teasing purple petals litter the brown grass. Anyone walking past would not notice them at all.

A slow shuffle of crunching salt on the cement approaches. Marcel stands a few feet away from me, looking into the field. For a moment I think that maybe, if I stand still, he won't be able to see me. It is only wishful thinking.

"Can you?" he asks.

"No. I cannot see it."

"I can't either."

Marcel keeps his eyes fixed on the grassy gap. I wonder what it is he has found now, and whether he is thinking of her.

I turn away from the clearing and toward the town. It glows like neon in the dim dusk light. Bright restaurant signs, slow headlights cruising, the occasional flicker of a streetlamp awakening for night. The top of the historic inn rises into the sky, dark and abandoned. A single light flickers in the top floor of the hotel. Perhaps the bathroom. Perhaps the wife.

Quercus

Emma Louise Gill

Emma Louise Gill (she/her) is a British-Australian speculative fiction writer, surviving on sunshine and coffee. Her words appear in Wyldblood Magazine, Where the Weird Things Are (Deadset Press), and Etherea Magazine, among others. She blogs at emmalouisegill.com and procrastinates on Twitter @ emmagillwriter. She greets every tree she sees. Sometimes they greet her back.

The oak tree outside my window ate my heart on Monday, and now it's turning golden even though it's spring. I think it's dying.

Fallen leaves pile into treasure overnight. Once, I'd have worn my kicking boots and made short work of the mountain. But I'm older now, past that, so I take my coffee out in the morning and squeeze my toes into the damp litter instead. Bitter steam curls into the mist, dissipating into day. Green and yellow finger-leaves cling to my bare feet like papier-mâché. I am become a simulacrum, a canvas for nature's whim. I turn my face to the canopy and ask for my heart's return. The oak laughs in a child's voice, and showers me with acorns.

I pour my coffee on its roots and retreat inside.

My brother comes by after lunch. He says I look like a pale sprite, and I reply he looks like a paladin, the knight he's named for. Dating has improved Gawain's temperament, though he could do better—and saying such things is what younger sisters are for. He leaves me a bottle of red wine, frozen lasagne, and ten quid, because that's what older brothers are for. I don't tell him about the tree development, but he glares at it on the way out.

On Thursday, the oak drops all its leaves at once. I walk to the newsagents under clear skies, and when I return all the branches are bare, like a brain with its nervous system exposed, dried out, black. All around it, the earth is stained the red of blood when a cut runs deep. We once kept chickens, and I remember that red seeping from a severed head, and my father's inflamed cheeks, and the fresher scarlet of the fox he killed. I think it's buried under the tree, actually.

Maybe that's when the oak got a taste for flesh.

I can't see a hole where my heart was before Monday. But I know the branch went right through me, a spear of ice and pain that wakes me up sweating every night. All week, I find splinters in my clothes, and my hair becomes thick, stringy, like tangled ivy. On Saturday, I drink the entire bottle of wine Gawain left and march outside under the swollen moon. The rest of the world sleeps in hushed peace, but the oak tree groans like my mother in labour, a sound I've never forgotten. Bats flit overhead, searching for insects with a chitter on the edge of hearing. I turn on the porch light for the moths and the bats and let them battle. *Nature is as nature does*, my father used to say. Then he'd take his shotgun and cast judgement.

The grass is wet from drizzle. Kneeling in the mulch beneath the oak, I dig my nails into cookie-dough earth and wonder if my baby brother is dying again. He's watched me from inside the tree all these years. I used to leave him small appeasements, but this time it's been months since the semester started and I only came back these holidays when I had nowhere else to go. The oak's trunk holds the story of my childhood: teeth and hair and blood, skin and tears and once, a baby bird. Stuffed inside the hollows he opened for me in the scarred bark. But these days all my gifts are words, most of them forlorn. Maybe that's why the tree ate my heart. It might as well be useful for something.

I know my baby brother's mad at me for poisoning our mother

with my blood: my antigens and his and hers were incompatible. It's why our father took a spade to soft dirt, planted the oak in our garden. I don't believe he knew of the tree's animosity, of the grief and hate its cells incubated. Of the dead child casting judgement on the living.

The oak grows faster than it should, but it was never just an oak, anyway.

Father lies there with Mother now, wrapped in my baby brother's roots: my family, our regrets, the bones of life leaching nutrients to create another.

"I love you," I say, and press my hands to scraggly bark. It scratches like a rough tongue, like those buried teeth have risen to the surface, tempted to bite. The bats swoop for moths as clouds kidnap the moon, and sap runs from the tree onto my fingers like sticky tears. It smells of sour vinegar and expired dreams.

A fox wakes me with a yip at dawn. It assesses me on my bed of broken twigs and fouled earth, its two eyes like burning embers boring into my wounds. My chest becomes a cavern, an icy void. Whatever it sees, the fox turns and runs, leaping over the back fence like a spirit or a demon, and the orange of its fur blends into the sunrise. A bright new leaf buds, unfurls, and detaches from my hair to fall in lazy spirals, buoyed by the breeze.

I call Gawain. Although it's early on a Sunday morning, he responds. I don't need to give an excuse. He brings his boyfriend and a borrowed chainsaw, and we say our goodbyes to the oak and the skeletons beneath its wings. Make a pile of firewood that will cure by winter.

An acorn grew in my palm last night. I hid it from Gawain, this secret in my hand. I'm going to feed it blood and bone and grow it in the sun. When my skin turns green like oak leaves in summer, it will be ripe.

Then I'll dig my toes into the ground and reach my branches up to the infinite sky.

The Oak Tree

Liz Baxmeyer

Liz Baxmeyer is a writer, musician, and visual artist living in Sacramento, CA, but originally from England. She is inspired by the environment, music, and folklore, especially where these things intersect. Her work is published or forthcoming in Beyond Words Literary Magazine, Wild Roof Journal, The Examined Life Journal, Syncopation Literary, and more. @lizbaxwrites

It was the cusp of winter, and every so often, the muted sound of a small icicle could be heard falling onto the frost-hardened ground with a glassy 'plink.' At first glance this almost impenetrable forest seemed to have no life in it, but if one looked closely enough, the warm breath of weasels and red foxes could be seen drifting up into the early morning air in thin wisps, and the scattered pines, which stood like velvet-green sentinels, tipped their crowns above the intoxicating mist as if to remind the world of their presence. But the creatures here were always starving, always hunting. Sometimes Dara would catch one, play with its tail, listen to its stories. Weasels have unique stories if you know how to hear them.

Dara sat at the base of the old oak tree alongside an overgrown path seldom trodden. Her small back rested against its rough, twisted trunk, and she played with the dirt between the tree's bonelike roots. Mud encrusted her fingernails and gave her an urchin-like appearance. Dara's face had the look of a snowdrop come too early, or a lily too late, never quite reaching full bloom, and her eyes were the hue of violet slate and gave those who looked at her a sense of unease–or wonder. She looked up to the sky and studied the sliver of broken, cantankerous light through untamed branches. She sang.

I went out to the old oak wood where the acorns scatter in droves

Where fledglings fall on softest mulch and the bluebells paint a road

There you said you loved me; you gave me a fox's tail

Oh, how I wore it round my neck like the Devil's bridal veil

You swore you'd always love me; a silver ring I'd see

And we made a promise good and true underneath the old oak tr–

Dara's singing was disrupted by faint, swift footsteps coming through the brush. They were getting closer with each stride. She darted behind the tree trunk and waited in silence in case it was someone dangerous fleeing a terrible deed, as was often the case so deep in these woods. Out here, there were many grim and obscure places to hide; one could conceal themselves for days without being discovered. When the creature emerged it didn't seem to be a criminal at all, but a woman, close to middle age, wearing shoes that were not designed for the heavily threaded terrain. The woman stopped in front of the huge oak tree and started picking at the ground with a stick, scurrying from one point to the next like a squirrel searching for its mushroom hoard. After a short time, and feeling more curious than threatened, Dara peeked out from her hiding place. The woman did not see her at first, still consumed by her search. Dara thought the whole scene was perfectly silly and couldn't help but let out a small giggle. The woman turned, startled.

"Who's there?" she called out, Dara's form still obscured in the graying light. The woman spun, stick in hand, as she tried to find a presence.

"Just me," Dara responded, promptly. "I didn't mean to scare you." She was sincere, but how does one appear from nowhere in the middle of a vast, dark wood without causing some alarm? "Honestly," she said, more softly.

The woman landed on Dara's unusual eyes and tried to ground herself. "How long have you been there? Are you spying on me?" she asked, wary of the silhouette with violet eyes in front of her.

"A minute, maybe?" Dara explained. "I wasn't trying to... I was already here. I'm sorry." She stepped into what little light there was.

The woman softened a little when she saw Dara's small form. "Isn't it a little strange for a young woman to be out here alone? You are alone?" she asked.

"Yes, quite alone." Dara gestured to the trees as if to confirm her statement.

"You do know this is a dangerous place? People have disappeared out here!" the woman warned.

"I know," she responded, "What's your name?"

The woman did not answer.

"I'm Dara."

The woman was still hesitant, but returned the offer of an introduction. "Then I suppose I'm Muriel."

"Muriel, are you looking for something?" Dara asked as she edged forward.

"Maybe," Muriel replied, backing away slightly, "How old are you?"

"I'm seventeen but perhaps beyond my years. That's what my father says, anyway. Or said. He is no longer of this world."

"Oh. I'm sorry... Well, I suppose if he were he would not have let you come out here all alone? And your mother?" Muriel took on a tone of pity.

"Died in childbirth. I never knew her," said Dara. She had obviously explained this many times.

"I am sorry for that."

"Was a long time ago," Dara reassured her. "Besides, these woods were not always this dark. This used to be a place for friends and lovers to come and walk on summer evenings; they'd tell each other tales under this oak tree!" She gestured upward.

"It's so dark and twisted!" Muriel noticed.

"I rather like it," Dara remarked as she approached the tree and clasped a low-hanging branch. "I think it's characterful. It knows itself. Doesn't try to be something it isn't."

"A matter of opinion, perhaps," Muriel replied, seemingly agitated. She was getting distracted from what she had come here for and was becoming fidgety. She launched back into her search with a refreshed sense of urgency. "Well, as soon as I find what I am looking for I'll be on my way." She paused and looked at Dara, "You should, too."

Dara continued her song while Muriel combed the clearing.

Oh the catkins glisten in the dew, their dancing tails do glow

Oh Weeping Will is mourning still and the sun does kiss him so

The Foxglove stands the tallest, all robed in white and red

Oh those who drink its nectar will surely end up dead.

"That song," Muriel cut in, "It's rather morbid, no?"

"Just an old folk song. They're nearly always about love or death, or both, you know. But there's often a lot of truth to them." Dara responded. "In a way I find them comforting."

"Folk songs make me uneasy. Too many stories about jilted women and ruthless men hunting innocent prey." Muriel shivered as she hacked at the spindled brush. It was getting harder to see, and she was becoming more and more nervous. After disturbing the foliage in almost every part of the small clearing, she sat down on the ground, defeated.

"I know it's here somewhere. I'm sure of it." She fought back tears. She didn't know what to do.

"Oh, tell me what you're seeking. I know I can help you." Dara approached Muriel closely for the first time.

"It's my coat," Muriel shared. "I know that sounds strange. But if I don't find it..." She stopped herself, still unsure about trusting this strange young woman. "I don't know what I'll do."

"I don't see a coat around here." Dara said. "So you left it? Where?"

"I didn't leave it. It was taken from me." Muriel replied as she started to shiver.

"May I ask why it means so much? It's just a coat."

"It's one of a kind. Seal's fur" Muriel explained. "I cannot return home to my family without it. And finding it means... it means I can escape him and finally go back to them." Her shiver turned into a light, whimpering sob.

"Who?" Dara inquired, now invested in Muriel's situation.

Muriel did not answer right away. The night had started to roll in like dark ink swirling in clear water. Muffled owls' hoots swelled in the branches close by, and a fox's screech punctuated from a distance. Nocturnal animals were beginning to hunt, and this was no longer a world for the living. Muriel was not inclined to stay much longer.

"My husband, he took it and buried it deep in the forest so I would not find it. I overheard him tell of its whereabouts while drinking with his brother last night; he becomes rather loose-tongued when he thinks I cannot hear him. Though he's usually more careful. So, this evening, I waited until he was drunk and then snuck from the house, but he will eventually notice I am gone, and he will know why. I never leave unless he bids me to, and he is not a forgiving man... I don't have much time." She raised her voice, "And I will not be strong or fast enough to escape him if I do not find my coat!" Muriel gasped. She had shared too much; her judgement foiled by her desperation.

Dara looked on, her eyes widening as if something had just occurred to her. She sang a different song:

There once was a hunter who laid with a maid, come ashore to dance in the dunes

As she played on the sand, her silver pelt he found, and he buried it under the moon, the moon

Yes he buried it under the moon.

When she noticed it gone, how she wept, how she mourned for her home in the wide open sea

This young hunter had trapped her upon the dry land, this poor Selkie no longer swum free

This poor Selkie no longer swum free.

Dara went on, "When a Selkie comes to shore in the night to dance in human form, there are those that will steal their seal's pelts, and when they do, the Selkie cannot return to their own world. They are trapped in human form, forced to belong the one who bound them when they truly wish to return to the salt and the wild waves."

"I don't know what you mean," said Muriel.

Dara stared at her. Muriel looked back, bewildered. She had been unveiled and was too desperate and defeated to endure the pretense. "Sometimes we fall in love; stay because we wish to... I was not so fortunate." Muriel planted herself at the base of the oak tree and gathered what constitution she had left. Something about it grounded her despite its eerie, distorted features. She bowed her head and sobbed again.

Dara comforted her the best she knew how. She sat by Muriel and patted her on the hand with her pale, dirt-laced fingers. "There, there," she cooed. She noticed strands of glimmering silver and shimmering gold in Muriel's hair that she had not observed before, remnants of the ocean, perhaps. Perhaps Selkies age in silver and gold as the moon reflects on the waves, night after night, until they become a part of the ancient sea from which they came, all shipwreck and mysticism. Muriel's eyes were a deep sapphire, and through tears, became little lagoons of their own. Dara decided that recognizing a magical creature was not that difficult if you looked hard enough. Besides, there was nearly always a song to guide you to the truth.

"I know what it is to be trapped." said Dara.

"You are only seventeen! How could you know what it is to be imprisoned like this?" Muriel snapped as she wiped away tears.

Dara rose and circled the trunk of the oak tree: "I was supposed to marry a young man once. The son of my father's friend. He was charming; called me his little ruby on account of the way I'd blush at a compliment. Difficult to picture now, I know." She looked to Muriel for a sign of confirmation. "He pledged to marry me under this tree."

"What happened?" asked Muriel, her tears now subsiding.

"As soon as a young lady by the name of Mary Connell came to town, he started to lose interest. Her father was much wealthier than mine; he owned silver mines, and she always presented herself with a sense of ease among men. I could not complete with that kind of woman." Dara reflected. "I was not important to him anymore. He became someone else entirely, and committed himself to pursuing her, leaving me in a state of perpetual unrest."

Dara was interrupted by heavy, fast paced footsteps coming through the woods from the same direction Muriel had arrived.

"Oh, no!" exclaimed Muriel. "It must be my husband! He must have figured out where I went." She was terrified.

"Here, come." Dara ushered Muriel behind the oak tree and pulled her into a small cavity in its trunk. Muriel had to squeeze her tall body through the exposed roots to enter the confining space, but there was just enough room for them both if they curled up and did not move. The footsteps became louder and more uneven as they approached the small clearing.

There was silence, then, a low, hostile voice called out, "Muriel?

Muriel!" Her husband. They heard him pace erratically around the clearing–perhaps, they assumed, to make sure he was truly alone. Then there came the metallic thud of a shovel in dirt.

"He sounds like an utter dream," Dara sneered.

"He's digging," Muriel whispered, Dara's sarcastic tone lost on her. Fear had taken over. "He'll find it and then I'll never escape! He'll be enraged with me!" As she turned to Dara she noticed her eyes had become faintly incandescent, like they'd summoned their own source of light from the inside. Dara was unresponsive, staring ahead as if in a trance. Muriel was too distracted by her own anxiousness over the figure outside to care to make any sense of it. Then, the digging sound stopped, and in the same stroke came a sudden swoop and an immense creaking and cracking, after which followed a more muffled and harrowing crunch akin to a carpenter's knuckles being broken under a hammer.

Dara, now released from her trance, turned to Muriel: "We can go out now."

"I dare not move!" Muriel insisted, trembling.

Dara went first, taking Muriel's hand as they unfettered themselves from the root-thick fingers of the tree.

Muriel scanned the scene, still utterly on edge. The ground was black aside from a small cocoon of light coming from an overturned lantern a few feet ahead of them. Then, her eyes were drawn up by a subtle movement just above the light's yellow-white orb.

"Wh-where did he go?" She asked as Dara went over to the lantern and lifted it into the air. Muriel gasped, in a state of horrified awe. Her husband hung about fifteen feet up in the tree, branches clenched around his neck and chest, crushing him in a jagged noose of warped branches. His eyes bulged and his body was limp; he looked much smaller than his ogre-like frame, entwined in the enormity of the tree. In his arms he held Muriel's pelt, all tattered and crusted in dried earth.

"The hunter becomes the hunted," said Dara, dryly, as she reached up and tugged the fur down from the dead man's grasp. "Here." She handed it to Muriel, still silent and still as a petrified sapling. "You're free."

"The tree... You're connected to it, aren't you? That's how you know what it is to be trapped," observed Muriel.

"I was not so strong as you. Your husband was unkind—even beastly in his pursuit for ownership—but my lover was an ambitious coward. After coaxing me here with the promise of a ring, finally, he lay me down, and slit my throat with another kind of silver. These woods have not seen starlight since." Dara paused; she could see Muriel's face becoming even more fearful.

"I—I thank you, Dara, but I must go now. The tide will roll out too far if I wait much longer. Take care," she bumbled. Muriel briefly looked up again at her dead husband, then back at Dara, then, facing the tree so as not to lose sight of either of them, stumbled backwards across the clearing, and down the path into the darkness.

As soon as she was sure she would not be followed, she turned on her heel and ran swiftly through the brush. Her awkward form, meant for swimming rather than running, did not stop for any sound or creature until she was out of the woods and across the dunes. Perhaps she did not stop until she launched her sleek form back into the undying waves and out to the silver-moon sea.

Dara sat down against the trunk of the oak tree as its contorted limbs swayed gently under the weight of its recent prey. A wisp of guilt passed momentarily through the air as she exhaled it into the ether, "No. It was worth it; she is free now," she whispered.

Yes you took your silver dagger and split my throat full sore

All for the pride of a lady whom you loved for her money more

And the tree she took great pity; she gave me arms and legs

She gave my spirit room to grow, and her roots became my bed

But I am awake and wondering beyond the open door

I have slept for a hundred years and I'll wait for a hundred more

So if you come this way now, beware of the old oak tree

Especially if you're a young man who cares only for a dowry

Yes if you come this way now beware of spirits three:

The woman scorned and never mourned, and the devil and the old oak tree;

The devil and the old oak tree.

THANK YOU TO OUR SUPPORTERS

Many thanks to our patrons and supporters, especially:

Wichael Tellez • Cathrin Hagey
Natalie Weizenbaum • Kate Boyes
Johanna Levene

Alina Kanaski • Jeffery Reynolds • Myz Lilith
D.M. Domosea • carol shoemake • Erik DeBill
Frederick Stark • Bonnie Warford • Felicia OSullivan
Salomao Becker • Anna O'Brien • Martin Cohen
J'nae Spano • Tory Hoke • S Klotz • Alex grehy
Rainer Fehrenbacher

Altaire Gural • Ana Wang • Lorna D Keach • smokestack
Lisa Short • Sian Jones • Kristina Saccone
Matthew Bennardo • BethOfAus • J. Askew
Dirck de Lint • Wanda • Karen Anderson
Charlotte Nash-Stewart • Suzanne Thackston
Jen G • Emily Anderson • Maria Haskins • GriffinFire

Want to see your name here? Become a patron!
patreon.com/lunastation

About the Cover Artist

Samantha Lee is a freelance landscape artist.

You can find more of her work at:

https://samanthalee.com

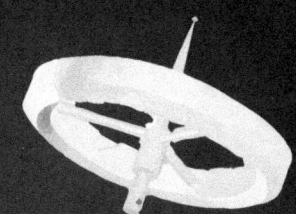

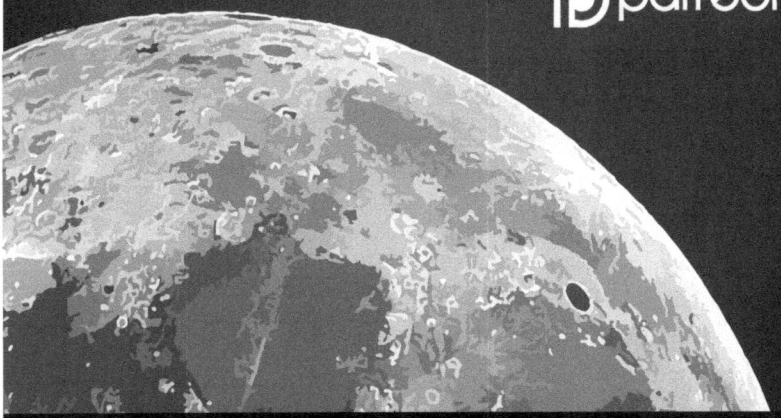